KU-541-950

Pigeon Fancying
in Leicestershire

Pigeon Fancying in Leicestershire

John Littlefair

The Book Guild Ltd

First published in Great Britain in 2019 by
The Book Guild Ltd
9 Priory Business Park
Wistow Road, Kibworth
Leicestershire, LE8 0RX
Freephone: 0800 999 2982
www.bookguild.co.uk
Email: info@bookguild.co.uk
Twitter: @bookguild

Copyright © 2019 John Littlefair

The right of John Littlefair to be identified as the author of this
work has been asserted by him in accordance with the
Copyright, Design and Patents Act 1988.

All rights reserved. No part of this publication may be
reproduced, transmitted, or stored in a retrieval system, in any form or by any means,
without permission in writing from the publisher, nor be otherwise circulated in
any form of binding or cover other than that in which it is published and without
a similar condition being imposed on the subsequent purchaser.

This work is entirely fictitious and bears no resemblance to any persons living or dead.

Typeset in Aldine401 BT

Printed and bound in Great Britain by CPI Group (UK) Ltd, Croydon, CR0 4YY

ISBN 978 1912575 954

British Library Cataloguing in Publication Data.
A catalogue record for this book is available from the British Library.

MIX
Paper from
responsible sources
FSC
www.fsc.org   FSC® C013604

To Nasreen, Robert and Philip

1

Lanfranco DeLuca, Mr DeLuca to friends and enemies alike, looked pensively out of the French windows of his study down the long drive which led to the Felton Road. It was lined by cypress trees which reminded him of the approach to the village near Naples where he was born and provided solace in his old age. Turning around, he studied a pigeon, busily pecking at some corn scattered over the green leather top of his desk. To the uninitiated this pigeon was very similar to any member of the species one might encounter while strolling around Trafalgar Square. Admittedly it looked in particularly good health and its walk had a touch of strutting arrogance, but otherwise it seemed to be a commonplace pigeon with two beady eyes, pink legs, a pair of wings and a tail. Its plumage was of the normal so-called ash red colour, and it would have taken the eye of a pigeon fancier to note the absence on its wings of the black bars, or mealies, that adorned most racing pigeons. This was an unusual variant called barless. However, DeLuca, champion breeder and racer, winner of the National on a record six occasions, was less concerned with the colour of his pigeon than its prowess as an athlete, for this was a king amongst racing pigeons. Winner of the Italian Derby, the Belgian South Road Annual and the English National, it had swept the board during its brief, but productive career. Now retired, it had been bought at considerable expense to take up stud duties. This paragon of the pigeon world, called in acknowledgement of his Italian origins Rosso Rummo, had cost Mr DeLuca ninety-five thousand pounds. At least, that was the advertised sum for insurance and tax purposes, although the amount of money that had changed hands had been about half that amount. He considered it a sound investment. With offspring fetching up to five thousand pounds each he would have been in profit within a couple of years, good health and normal sex life permitting.

DeLuca looked up from the pigeon and glowered at Arthur, his loft manager.

'What do you mean he doesn't like girls?' he said crossly. 'Are you trying to tell me I've bought a poofter pigeon? You must be joking. That bird cost me a fortune'.

'I've tried pairing 'im up a dozen times,' Arthur said in a broad Yorkshire accent. 'He always returns to the same pigeon, a blue cock. If I put them apart the blue one starts fighting and Rosso here goes into a sulk and won't eat.'

'You must be doing something wrong.'

Arthur bridled.

'I think I've been in this game long enough to know what's what,' he replied testily. 'It 'appens occasionally. Remember that bird you got from your brother. Must be twenty year ago or more now. That one was the same.'

'I could have killed my brother over that,' DeLuca observed ruefully. 'Always up to tricks. I couldn't show my face in the club for a year. All the same, are you sure that other bird is a male? Perhaps you've got the sex wrong. You know how hard it can be sometimes. I think we should get a second opinion. Give that man who was featured in *Pigeon World* last week a ring. What was his name? Stephen Larcher? He's getting a good reputation for himself. Get both birds checked out.'

Arthur was a stocky man of nearly seventy with a phlegmatic countenance that belied a volatile manner and a thin skin. He had been the loft manager for the Queen until he had been lured away by DeLuca twenty-five years ago by the promise of a doubling of his salary and access to the best birds. For nearly forty years he had held, with some justice, the reputation of being the finest pigeon man in the country. He was especially proud of his unrivalled expertise in pigeon psychology and had written, or rather had written for him, what was regarded as the definitive work on the subject. However, he was beginning to show his years, although he wouldn't admit this to anyone, least of all himself. His eyesight in particular was poor and the last two seasons hadn't been as successful as usual. He was acutely aware of whispers in the pigeon world that age was catching up with him and that there would soon be a vacancy at the DeLuca loft. In most situations a modest man, when it came to pigeons he could be haughty and arrogant, especially if his judgement was called into question. At DeLuca's suggestion of a second opinion his ruddy complexion, the combined result of an outdoor life and a fondness for the product of the local Oakwood Brewery, deepened by several shades. Drawing himself up to his full five foot six inches, he gave a restrained snort.

'Do you think I can't tell the difference between a hen and cock?' he said in a tone that indicated any man who was of that opinion would be invited outside to settle the issue in the traditional manner.

DeLuca was not the sort of employer who liked to be challenged. An autocratic man, he expected unquestioning obedience from those within his power. He was, however, a devoted pigeon fancier and gained much of his enjoyment in life from this sport. Aware of his own limitations he had long recognised that in Arthur, when it came to pigeons, he had a giant amongst men. It was only when Arthur had joined him that his phenomenal success had started, the combination of Arthur's ability and DeLuca's money making a formidable team. He had so far managed to thwart the several attempts to coax Arthur away, but this had only been possible by an uncomfortable reversal in the roles of master and servant. When it came to matters concerning pigeons, Arthur's word held sway. Any attempt by DeLuca to impose his opinion on training regimes, breeding lines and nutritional requirements had been met by contemptuous resistance that brooked no interference. Long ago DeLuca had accepted that if he wanted to keep winning he had to subjugate himself to this tantrum-prone, opinionated and often insufferable Yorkshireman. To his credit, Arthur had never let him down and DeLuca had rarely, if ever, known him to be wrong on any matter to do with pigeons.

'Of course not Arthur, of course not,' DeLuca said hurriedly, realising his error. 'It's just that, as you know, it can be very difficult to sex a bird and I thought—'

'I'll thank you not to think sir if you don't mind. I'll have you remember that I was Captain of the Queen's Flight. Do you think it likely that Her Royal Highness would employ a man who couldn't even tell the sex of a pigeon? If you reckon I'm no longer up to my job I'll be on my way. There are a number of other people who still think I have summat to offer, I can tell you.'

With difficulty DeLuca restrained his anger at his employee's impertinence. If he had heard that refrain about being Captain of the Queen's Flight once, he had heard it a hundred times. He had crossed swords with Arthur only a month ago over a little matter of a herbal remedy for a bird with an infected foot, and the discussion about the virtues of conventional versus alternative medicine had become quite heated. DeLuca, who thought it unlikely that at his age Arthur could find another job, had vowed that the next time he was rebuffed, he would call Arthur's bluff and sack him. He was summoning up the courage to dismiss the man, when he recalled the occasion five years ago when tempers had flared and Arthur had temporarily left the establishment. It had been awful. Half the birds went down with food poisoning, the new man managed to set fire to one of the lofts and a sparrowhawk had eaten his best racing bird. He had been forced to beg Arthur to return with a pay rise and a share in the profits. He shuddered at the recollection.

'All right Arthur. I've never known you to be wrong I'll admit that. Try again though can't you? Change the feed. Maybe he's feeling homesick. Get some Italian corn. Moving home can upset a bird. Play some Verdi. Do something. Oh, and Arthur,' he continued, as Arthur picked up the recalcitrant bird.

'Aye.'

'Not a word to anyone you understand? If this gets out I'll be a laughing stock from here to Brindisi. Not a word now you hear?'

2

'You need to pull yourself together,' Louise said briskly.

Joe, resisting the urge to defend himself against this harsh instruction, smiled wanly, but Louise was not to be brushed off so easily.

'No, I mean it. Look at you. It's been a whole month since you lost your job and you're still dripping with self-pity. If nothing else we need to pay the mortgage. I'm not going to go on keeping you in the style to which you've become accustomed, that's for sure.'

Joe abstractly noticed a Sugar Puff, which, escaping from his spoon, had skied down the slopes of his chest into his lap, leaving a trail of milk droplets in its wake. He picked up the piece of wheat and, after studying it briefly in the light from the kitchen window, popped it into his mouth. He then wiped the milk into the wool of his crimson dressing gown, leaving a distant stain.

'I've still got two months of redundancy money left.'

Louise came over and ran her fingers through his hair.

'I know that getting sacked knocked you for six sweetheart, but you've got to get out there and show them. You're a brilliant writer, you could get a job tomorrow if you set about it.'

'I wasn't sacked I was reconfigured.'

'I know. Sorry. Look. I've got to go. Remember we're going round to Susan's tonight for a meal. I'll meet you there. Will you bring a bottle of wine? The Sauvignon in the fridge will do. Oh, and make sure you pay the phone bill and we need some milk and cat food. And do be a dear and plant that thing Mum sent for your birthday. She is bound to ask when she rings up and she always knows when I'm lying.' Then, with a brushed kiss, she was gone.

Joe stared mournfully at the cereal packet wondering whether to help himself to another bowl. It was his experience that Sugar Puffs flattered to deceive, so that by mid-morning the stomach began to rumble uncomfortably. He was however, unable to summon the energy to lift the packet. He had been feeling like this for a while now. Lifeless, everything too much of an effort. He clearly recognised that having just turned thirty-three, getting out of bed should not be the herculean task it had become. He wondered if he was allergic to something.

Recalling the events that had resulted in his enforced period of leisure, it crossed his mind that his recent dismissal from his job as deputy editor of *Retail Monthly* could have something to do with it. There was no doubt it had been a body blow. When his friend and colleague Kay Welden had left the editorship of the paper, it had been widely assumed, at least by him, that he would ease comfortably into her chair without any fuss. Not that he saw this as a great career move. When he had embarked on his life as a journalist, after obtaining a good 2:2 in English from the University of West Anglia, he had thought he would be destined for greater things than reporting from the latest skirmish in supermarket price wars. Then again *RM*, as its was known to the cogniscenti, wasn't so bad. It was after all one of the least loss-making magazines in the Heskey publishing empire and was on the brink of getting its on line offer sorted out. Joe had to admit that he may not have been the most dynamic of journalists. He enjoyed his lunch hour as much as the next man and his laissez-faire attitude to having his phone both switched on and charged up hadn't helped with the twenty-four hour news frenzy that had invaded even the sleepiest corners of the press world. Nonetheless, he had been confident that after five years of loyal service he was ready to take on the challenge of the editorship. He felt he deserved it. Sadly, it turned out this was not a view shared by management. Completely out of left field, they had appointed some twenty-five-year old with virtually no experience of retail. What did he know about the crisis in out-of-town shopping malls or the effect (admittedly very little), of business rates on charity shops? All this wet-behind-the-ears proto-scribbler had to commend him was a charming smile, a ready wit and a rugby blue from Oxford. OK, and a first class degree and a masters from an elite journalism school. Joe was keenly aware that he hadn't taken the news with particularly good grace. There was no doubt that his snide remark suggesting he'd got the job because his dad and the owner were both members of the the same club did not help his cause, not least because it turned out he had misheard his source. One was in Brook's and the other in Buck's.

It was on the following Monday that he had received a memo stating that the editorial staff of the magazine was to be re-configured and could he clear his desk by lunchtime? Reconfigured indeed – why didn't they just say he was sacked and be done with it? He wished in retrospect that he had been more dignified about his departure. Pleading on his knees to give him another chance had been a big mistake. He didn't know what had come over him. Shock, he assumed. It had been meant as a sort of joke, but the imperious way in which the new editor had brushed him aside had been humiliating.. The image still made his cheeks burn with shame.

He started to feel the pain that had been bothering him grip his chest. He was ill. No doubt about it. It didn't t Louise was so unsympathetic, he thought. That his partner of three years, far from offering support, had become impatient as soon as he entered a rough patch, was disappointing. She failed to realise how much stress the reconfiguration had caused. It was true, as she didn't tire of pointing out, that her life was also very stressful and carried the additional strain of having to get up in the morning, but he felt there was still room for a little empathy.

Joe bleakly contemplated the day ahead. Shopping, cleaning, the phone bill, gardening, a trip to the doctor's. Endless chores and all pointless. After all, the world would hardly stop spinning if he didn't get the clematis in before her mum phoned. It occurred to him, not for the first time that month, how unnecessary his life had become. If he was suddenly called to higher things, apart from a few tears and an hour or two of extra work for the Registrar of Births Deaths and Marriages, the world would be largely unaffected. His life had existed through activity and now he had nothing to do. No deadlines to meet, articles to write, meetings to attend. Nobody to interview and no one to go to lunch with.

He had almost decided to go back to bed for a few hours when the doorbell rang. It was the postman with a registered letter. The cream envelope, postmarked Leicestershire, was addressed in typescript to Mr Joseph Landseer. He signed for the letter, which he put on the hall table, and leant against the open door watching the postman amble down the street, his fluorescent postbag banging rhythmically against his leg. Joe lived in the ground-floor flat of a three storey Victorian terraced house in the southern part of Brixton. Louise and he had bought it two years ago when they had started living together. It represented value for money at a time when the riots were a distant memory and Brixton was yet again up-and-coming. The road was adjacent to one of the more notorious estates in South London, a fact of which they had been unaware at the time. However, crime against either property or person had been infrequent, although a degree of perspective was required to appreciate this. To a resident of Middle England, once a month might seem quite enough to have the peace disturbed by the police doing house-to-house enquiries, but compared to the Stockwell Road Estate, Stensfield Road was a crime-free zone.

It was a lovely late-winter day. The sky was azure and the air was as crisp and fresh as it ever got in London. There was nothing to indicate the disharmony that sometimes spoiled the convivial if spirited ambience of the road. The impromptu garage that had excited Louise into writing increasingly desperate letters to the environmental health department of the local council had not yet started work. The blood stain in the road, the result of an unequal duel between a feral cat and a speeding car, had been mostly washed away by the previous night's rain. Last but not least, the police had thoughtfully removed the markings that indicated the site of a near-fatal stabbing when a man on a community care programme had attacked a young woman after she had been unable to direct him to Nazareth. The street's residents had reassured themselves with the thought that this was the sort of motiveless crime that could have happened anywhere, although it was curious how often it seemed to happen in Brixton. Joe, in his sombre mood, wondered whether, despite the fun involved in going to the clubs, theatres and cafes of booming London, there might be better places to live.

While he was pondering this point, a door opened on the opposite side of the street and a middle-aged black man appeared, dressed in vest and braces which held up a pair of pin-stripe trousers. He waved cheerily at Joe. 'All right?' he called.

Joe waved back. Freddy, colloquially called Mr Green Van because of a large green van which was parked permanently outside his house, was a self-appointed, one-man neighbourhood [e spent much of his time looking out through his net for unwelcome intruders. On several occasions he had apprehended representatives of the local youth, who he accused, – justly or not it was rarely very clear – of intent to break and enter. On occasions he could be a little overzealous. Only last month he had attracted the attention of Brixton's police regarding juvenile assault, and some years ago a fight had developed when the father of one accused youngster had taken the law into his own hands. Even more disturbingly, at least for the upwardly mobile members of the street's community, at least one house sale had faltered when Freddy had offered his security services to the prospective purchaser.

Chased back into the hall by a waft of cool morning air, Joe shut the door and picked up his letter. It was from a Mrs Morgan, a solicitor in Felton, Leicestershire, informing him that his great-aunt had died two days ago. As her executor Mrs Morgan had arranged the funeral for the next day, a Friday. It requested that Mr Landseer attend the reading of the will after the funeral.

Joe's immediate response was one of guilt. He had neglected his great-aunt in recent years. He was, as far as he knew, her only living relative in Britain. A spinster, unable to find a husband in the aftermath of the Great War, she had brought up Joe's orphaned mother when her younger sister had died in childbirth and Joe's grandfather, a merchant seaman, had been killed in the early years of the Second World War. As his parents had lived in the Far East for much of their lives, Joe had spent many school holidays with his Aunt Florence, until in his teens he was old enough to stay with school friends or make the long journeys east to Hong Kong and Singapore. He had happy memories of those rural summers, but had visited his aunt less often since reaching adulthood. She had become increasingly eccentric and cantankerous, although in good health. He wondered if the solicitor had written to his mother, although he couldn't see her making the trip from Spain. Joe rang the solicitor to confirm the arrangements and got dressed. At last he felt some purpose in his life, even it was just to bury a relative.

'You spent a lot of time talking to Susan tonight,' Louise said, her tone tinged with suspicion.

Joe watched as she undressed, holding onto the mantelpiece of the Victorian fireplace in their spacious bedroom as she removed one of her red high-heeled shoes. He had enjoyed the dinner party. Susan, the hostess, had been particularly friendly towards him and he had drunk sufficient wine to feel witty and urbane. On the way back in the taxi he had been indulging in a day dream about the possibility that he might inherit some money from his aunt. Musing about what he might do with a few thousand pounds, he admired the curve of Louise's bare arm as she peeled off her tights. A glimpse of her breast aroused more than glimmer of sexual excitement, his ardour already sensitised by the short skirt Susan had been wearing.

'Well?'

'Well what?'

'You haven't been listening to a word I've been saying, have you?'

Joe struggled to remember what Louise had asked him. He wondered if he'd had a little more to drink than he'd thought.

'Susan,' Louise said impatiently. 'She was flirting with you.'

'That's not true.'

'Yes it is. You spent all night talking to her.'

'I was sitting next to her,' Joe replied.

'And why was that?' Louise said, implying evidence of a conspiracy. 'We never talk. When was the last time we had a proper conversation rather than just discussing the shopping or paying bills? I don't think you love me any more. You're all wrapped up in yourself since you lost your job. What were you talking about anyway?'

'She noticed that I wasn't looking too good, so I was telling her about my visit to the GP. Then we got onto to her latest boyfriend. The doctor. They've parted company. He was always working apparently. Either that or falling asleep at crucial moments in their sex life.'

'I didn't know she and Tom had split up. No wonder she was making eyes at you. No man is safe with her around. She's lusted after you ever since that fling you had.'

'I thought she was one of your best friends.'

'That doesn't stop her being public enemy number one when she's unattached.'

'Well, she was very sympathetic about my chest pains,' Joe said, his tone clearly indicating that others in the more immediate vicinity were showing less concern than they might.

'All right,' Louise said wearily. 'What did the doctor say? All due to stress I expect. Probably recommended a holiday in the country.'

'He did actually. How did you guess?'

'That's what he said to Anne Selwyn, you know, at Number 37, when she went to him about her headaches. Mind you, she turned out to have a brain tumour.'

'That's very reassuring.'

'I told you it was just a matter of pulling yourself together. As for a trip into the country, you know what I think about that. As far as I'm concerned, the great English landscape is populated by creepy-crawlies, dunderheads on tractors who think that Francis Bacon is a breed of pig, and upper-class twits who bray like the donkeys they ride about on. And it's so dull. Simply nothing to do. I don't know why people go on about it, the countryside. I wish they could concrete over the lot and have done with it.'

'You won't be coming with me to Leicestershire then?' Joe said with commendable insight.

'Wild horses wouldn't drag me. Are you going to get anything do you think?'

'Doubt it. She'll leave it all to Mum I expect, or a charity. She was potty about wildlife and stuff. Not that there will be much to leave. The place was in ruins as I remember it.'

'Oh, I don't know. People will buy anything these days if you call it a cottage and get a few roses climbing up the wall. The world is full of suckers.'

3

Felton was a moderate-sized market town in East Leicestershire, situated at the southern end of the Vale of Belvoir. Like the rest of East Leicestershire and Rutland, the Vale was a patchwork of farmland and small villages, many of which still boasted a country pub and village green. Superficially at least, it resembled the image of a bucolic England beloved of tourist boards, feeding on a mirage of country life that largely ended with the war. If the over-sprayed grassland and cornfields were in reality green deserts, and if the quilt of fields were on alternate years knitted in yellow or blue, depending on the colour of the European subsidy, at least the hedges were generally intact and the fields mainly of human scale. Even after the hunting ban estate agents were partial to describing country properties in the area as being in the 'heart of hunting country'. This claim was not without justice, for it lay at the confluence of the territories of three famous hunts, the Quorn, the Cottesmore and the Belvoir. The hunting fraternity had shrugged off the change in the law and continued to regularly take over the country roads with their pantechnicon horse transports and binoculared hunt followers. Whether their activities were in defiance or in deference to the law of the land was a matter for debate. What was not for debate was the irrelevance of the hunt to the local economy. Market towns like Felton need more calories than can be gained from chasing hares and foxes to their gory death. The closure of the last deep coal mine in the Midlands a decade earlier had been an economic blow, and many townsfolk worked in the hospitals or universities in Leicester and Nottingham. However farming and Felton's main employer, Purrfect Pet Foods, kept the local economy in good heart and the several new housing estates ensured the town centre bustled with young families on market day.

Felton's main claim to fame was a certain type of pork pie made to a unique recipe since 1851. It was characterised by an outer coat of thick golden pastry and a generous lining of glutinous sauce. The pies looked so good that the purchaser was often tempted on leaving the shop to take an impromptu, pre-lunch sampling. In hot weather this often caused some difficulties, for as the jelly became less viscous, it had a tendency to dribble atavistically down the chin, especially when too large a bite was taken. Then the glutton, with hands full with multiple shopping bags, could be observed gyrating his or her tongue and lower jaw in a vigorous manner, attempting to scoop back the goblets of fat, an operation referred to colloquially as the Felton chin-wag.

Between Felton, with its Norman influences and Roman Leicester, there were a number of villages, scattered at intervals along the River Wreake, whose names, all ending in –by, the Norse for 'place', were evidence of a Viking influence. Joe's great-aunt had lived just outside one of these, Freasby, and it was in the village church that her funeral was to take place. Freasby was a picturesque village, set on a small promontory overlooking the river, which lay to the south. Half a mile further to the south was the East-West coast railway, and just beyond that, a busy road that ran between Felton and Leicester. The village was comprised of old farmworkers' cottages, converted farmhouses, some grander residences once belonging to minor gentry, but now occupied by lawyers and doctors from the city; and a small mansion called, in the plain way common to Leicestershire, the Manor House. The older houses were all built in the yellowed local ironstone and some retained their original thatching. Here and there, evidence of a contemporary culture could be seen in the large brick bungalow, complete with matching double garage, built awkwardly in the garden of an older house, whose owner had been prepared to sacrifice his view to take advantage of booming house prices in rural locations. Main Street ran south-west through the centre of the village and contained the majority of the commercial activities, namely a shop with sub-post-office, the Fox and Hounds public house, and a small garage. Halfway through the village, heading north-east, a right turn took you into Church Street. After a few hundred yards the lane opened onto the village green, on the edge of which was a pond, home to a pair of mallards and an occasional Canada goose on its way to Rutland Water. At the point where Church Street ended, a majestic large-leafed lime stood in silent guard of the village traditions. In its shadow sheltered the Agricultural Inn, a pub of similar vintage to the tree and by some, equally hallowed.

The taxi which brought Joe from Leicester dropped him at the end of Church Street. He looked across the green to the small Norman church, its churchyard fenced by black iron railings. The day was overcast and promised rain. He buttoned up his second-hand tweed overcoat, bought from a charity shop on Brixton High Street, shivering as he encountered the biting wind that blew down Church Street. Looking at his watch and reassured that he wasn't late, he walked over to the church. He could see a knot of mourners by the door, stamping the damp off their feet and exchanging pleasantries. Reluctant to introduce himself to strangers, he lingered on the path reading the names on the headstones. He wondered where his aunt was to be buried. She came from an old Freasby family and he vaguely remembered talk of a family plot. He had only been to one other funeral, that of his younger brother who had died of meningitis aged four. Unwilling to revive that memory, he considered waiting outside until the service was over, but then a gust of wind and an awareness that his feet, wet from the grass, were getting cold, persuaded him to take refuge from the elements.

The church was simply decorated, with plain stone walls and worn pews. A few flowers adorned the nave and a threadbare red carpet led up to the altar. Most of the stained glass was gone, but a single window in the chapel remained, resplendent in a multicoloured agony of crucifixion. A single bell began its doleful peal. Joe took a deep breath of the musty air and took a seat halfway down the aisle. There were about fifteen other mourners, scattered in ones and twos through the body of the church, apart, as is the way of the English on formal occasions. His visits to his aunt had been brief in recent years and he did not know many of her friends. He smiled at a man of about seventy seated a few rows away who he recognised and received a nod in return. Walter Bramley, who was sitting with his wife, had managed Joe's aunt's land, and together with his wife had looked after her in recent years. Across the aisle to the left of Joe, seated next to a younger woman, was a well-built, prosperous-looking man of about sixty with the ruddy cheeks and the plate-like hands of a farmer. This man he recognised as Fred Carter, a man who owned land next to his aunt's. Joe thought his aunt had enjoyed some sort of feud with him, but he supposed they must have made up. The woman was dressed smartly but comfortably in a black woollen coat over a well cut grey suit. She had dyed blonde hair. As she returned Joe's stare he realised that she was about his age, although her features, spoiled by cigarettes, looked older. There was a closed, hard-edged note to her expression that was more than just boredom. She gave him a cool, almost hostile look, before turning back to face the altar.

The organ started and pallbearers from an undertaker's in Felton carried in the coffin. Joe's mind wandered during the short service. Although he rarely went to church he was not hostile to its rituals, especially in churches such as this, whose traditions stretched back through the ages. Joe was attracted to the past, and as the vicar incanted her verses he imagined the lives of the people whose names were inscribed on the walls and floor. The vicar was new to the parish and hadn't known his aunt. The tribute was short, though not without taste, and then it was time for Joe to follow the coffin out into the churchyard where his aunt was laid to rest next to her parents. He watched as the earth fell onto the coffin and said his silent farewells.

'You must be Mr Landseer.'

He turned around to see a frosty-faced woman of about fifty, dressed in a sombre tweed suit and carrying a black umbrella which she proceeded to unfold, a cold drizzle having started.

'Jean Morgan, your aunt's solicitor,' she said, offering a firm handshake.

'How do you do?' Joe said politely.

'I need to read you the will,' she said bluntly. 'Shall I give you a lift to my office in Felton?

'There isn't a wake then?' he asked.

'Not that I am aware of. I don't believe she had many friends,' Mrs Morgan said, with a slight wave of her umbrella to indicate the small band of attendees, most not long from their own day of reckoning, huddled together against the rain. 'I didn't think a party would be appropriate, but of course, not being a member of the family, I may have misjudged matters.'

Joe recognised the criticism implicit in her remark and felt a pang of guilt that he had not done more to help with organising the funeral. 'Perhaps we could all go for a drink or something.' he suggested lamely.

'That would be awkward. I have meetings all afternoon,' she said firmly, her lips pinching with suppressed irritation. 'I believe I did say straight after the funeral.'

'Yes, of course,' Joe conceded, taking a dislike to the woman. 'I'll just say hello to Walter Bramley. Which is your car?'

She pointed to a blue Renault parked by the church gate.

As Joe went over to Walter and his wife, Mrs Morgan was joined by Fred Carter.

'Mornin' Jean. Right sort of weather for a funeral.'

'I didn't think you and Miss Chevanage were on speaking terms.'

'We were the best of enemies, but I find a certain satisfaction in the funerals of my opponents. Anyway, I wanted to have a word with you.'

'Oh yes?' she said cautiously.

'Who inherits?'

'You know I can't tell you that.'

'Come on. We know each other too well for that high-and-mighty stuff. You don't mean to tell me that you are worried about passing on a bit of information that will be common knowledge by the end of the week?'

'It would be highly irregular. In any case, why do you want to know?' she asked curiously.

'Because I want the property. Simple as that. I'm prepared to pay a fair price for it. There would be something in it for you if you helped me.'

'How much for me?'

'A couple of hundred.'

Jean snorted.

'Five then, for a bit of information, a good word put in and a deal done. Quite a bargain, I reckon.'

Jean saw Joe waiting by the car. 'I've got to go. What do you want more land for anyway? You must have over a thousand acres by now'

'Fifteen hundred and sixty to be exact,' he replied proudly, 'but you can never have too much land.'

Jean started to walk towards her car.

'Well?' Carter asked.

'He gets it,' she said, nodding in the direction of Joe. 'Gets the lot.'

4

DeLuca picked up the telephone and dialled, drumming his fingers impatiently on the desk while he waited for a response.

'Peter? Where on earth have you been? I've been trying to get you all week. I want you over here right now,' he ordered. 'I don't care if you are meeting the pope for lunch, you get over here. It's about that bloody bird you bought for me. I can't talk over the phone. Just get here pronto, right?'

Half an hour later Peter Garibaldi was ushered into DeLuca's study by the butler, Sims. Peter was a sharp-suited man in his late thirties, with a taste for expensive wines, red Ferraris and the gambling tables. He was a partner in a firm of Leicester solicitors which had been started by his father Marco who, like DeLuca, had come to England after the war as a teenager looking for work and had stayed on. Whereas DeLuca had started an ice-cream business, moving rapidly from a single van to a fleet and then making his fortune in property during the early 70s, Peter's father had gone to university, obtained a law degree and set up his own business. This had flourished, in part through the work put his way by his friend DeLuca. Peter, although generally competent, was shy of long hours and, unlike his immigrant father, not averse to cutting corners.

'Mr DeLuca, you look the picture of health. I don't know how you manage it.' In fact DeLuca was distinctly grey at the gills, but Peter was not the sort of man to point out the shortcomings of his clients. 'And how's Angela? Blooming I hope.'

The two men shook hands.

'Well I don't feel like a picture and as for my daughter its just one thing after another. She's only seventeen and she wants to go out every night instead of studying for her exams. To be honest with you Peter, she needs a mother. She has never been the same since Laura died. I'm too old to keep up with her. Serves me right for getting married so late. She has been very odd recently. Temperamental. Must be her age, I suppose. I hope she's not got into trouble with any man. I want my daughter to be intact when she marries. If I catch anyone playing around with her,' he said with sudden ferocity, 'I'll feed his balls to my pigeons.'

Peter, who had first-hand knowledge that DeLuca's daughter was no longer a virgin, flinched. He knelt down to pick up a piece of corn from the Persian rug in order to distract attention from a spasm of discomfort as he recalled his brief fling with Angela. He had known it was a mistake at the time, but he hadn't been able to resist. He felt a stirring in his loins as he recalled their first time a year ago when he had driven her into the country for a picnic. Lying down in the sun, she had suddenly stripped to her underwear, exposing her firm young breasts and long tanned legs to his lustful gaze. She had seduced him, he thought defensively. He was glad it had petered out after a couple of months. The risk of being caught by her father unnerved him. The anxiety had even started to affect his performance, a most worrying development. Their parting had been amicable; in fact he had gained the distinct impression that she had begun to find him boring. He had even wondered if he was being used to raise the interest of another of her suitors.

She certainly hadn't been in love with him. Anyway, that was nearly a year ago. Reassured he put the corn in his pocket and straightened up. Smoothing his trousers he looked at DeLuca. *Old boy needs a holiday,* he thought.

'Still,' DeLuca continued, 'that's not what I asked you over for. We have a problem with the pigeon.'

'Rosso?'

'What other bastard pigeon do you think I have spent a small fortune on recently?' DeLuca asked irritably.

Peter shrugged. *Sarcastic sod* he thought. *I don't know why I put up with him. He should show me some respect.* Then he remembered that most of his income came though DeLuca's various business interests and smiled placatingly.

'What's the problem?' Peter asked urbanely.

'What's the problem? What's the problem?' DeLuca nearly shouted. 'The problem, my friend, is that you have spent fifty thousand of my hard-earned cash on a stud pigeon whose chance of fertilising an egg is about as good as winning the lottery.'

'But he was checked out. He's fertile, unless the vet screwed up.'

'It's not his fertility that's the problem, we haven't got that far yet. It's his inclination. As we speak, Rosso is trying to hump Sam rather than Samantha. He's a bloody homosexual. He likes boys.'

'Well I never. I didn't know pigeons could swing the other way,' Peter said, faintly amused.

'Well you don't know much do you, and you can wipe that bloody smirk off your face. The point is, does the insurance cover it?'

'I'll have to take a look at the policy,' Peter said cautiously, 'but I think there may be a difficulty there. If you remember, because we knew he was fertile, we didn't insure him for infertility. It was an extra two thousand a year and you asked me to cut that clause out. Poisoning, theft, drowning, all covered. Homosexuality? Probably not.'

DeLuca glared at Peter.

'I don't remember telling you to go short on the insurance.'

'Well you did,' Peter said irritably. *Serve the old skinflint right*, he thought, although he was uncomfortably aware that he had still charged DeLuca for that extra clause. Still, he was confident enough that he had buried the evidence sufficiently deep in the accounts to escape detection.

'Terrific,' DeLuca said morosely. 'So what are you going to do about it? That bird is worthless unless it breeds. Worse still, I won't be able to show my face when this gets out, and get out it will. Arthur can't keep a secret beyond his second drink, and in any case people will be expecting offspring. Well? Say something.'

Peter felt it was unfair to blame him. He set up deals and negotiated prices. He couldn't be expected to supervise the mating habits of every pigeon he came across.

'I don't think you can blame me,' he replied lamely.

'Oh, don't you? Well, I've got news for you. I can, and I do. I've been set up on this one. Don't tell me Alfonso didn't know about it. I wondered why I got it so cheap. All that stuff about him selling up and retiring was crap. He's laughing at me right now. Come to think of it,' he continued, an idea suddenly striking him, 'isn't Alfonso's cousin getting married to Cosimo's eldest, Danny?' He struck the desk with his fist, making Peter wince. 'That's it. My brother is behind this. It's just the bastard sort of thing he would do. You're not in on this, are you?' He looked intently at Peter, who shifted his eyes to the carpet.

'No, of course not. What do you take me for?'

'A lily-livered, incompetent, lazy good-for-nothing, who is a disgrace to his father, if you want to know. And don't give me that look. I only keep my business with you for his sake. Look after you he said when he died, and I do my best, but I swear if I ever catch you double-crossing me I'll…'

'Feed my balls to the pigeons?' Peter offered wearily.' God, how he hated this man sometimes. *Still, beggars can't be choosers* he thought. 'Look, I had nothing to do with it and I can't believe your brother did either. It's probably just a simple mistake. I'll take another look at the insurance, may be we can claim under sickness or something.'

'And if we can't? In any case, that won't help with my reputation.'

'I can't believe anyone will worry about it,' Peter said reassuringly. 'These things happen.'

'Not to me they don't. You don't know the pigeon world. They hate me out there. A poor immigrant coming out on top, winning all their prizes, rubbing their faces in their second-rate training methods. They will humiliate me, and at the front of the pack will be Cosimo with a big fat smile all over his face. No, we must do something.'

'We could have him kidnapped?' Peter said jokingly.

DeLuca looked intently at Peter. 'Yes, we could,' he replied thoughtfully. 'That's the first sensible thing you've said. Get someone to kidnap the bird – we are insured for that aren't we? Send a ransom note and then kill it. The insurance people pay up and the problem is solved. As the bird is insured for ninety-five thousand we even make a nice profit. That will take the smile off Cosimo's face. Brilliant Peter. Perhaps you aren't such a bad lad after all.' DeLuca's grumpy expression was transformed into a cheerful smile of bonhomie.

Peter looked aghast.

'Let me get this right. You want me to kidnap one of your stupid birds, just so you won't be embarrassed at the Pigeon Fanciers' Ball? Well, you can stick that. It's against the law, that sort of thing you know. Defrauding the insurance company, wasting police time. We could even be done for cruelty to animals. I'd be finished. I might have to go to prison.'

'Don't be stupid Peter. The police are hardly likely to

mount a major crime investigation over a stolen pigeon, and since when have you been so squeamish about insurance scams? I seem to remember you handled that fire in John Webb's warehouse without too many qualms. It's beautiful. I get out of trouble, it's one in the eye for my brother, and we make a profit on the deal. I tell you what. You organise everything and I will give you half the profit. Twenty thousand quid. That will come in handy no doubt. Help with those gambling debts of yours.'

How did the old bastard know about that, Peter wondered? As for this obsession with his brother Cosimo, it was madness.

'And if I don't help you?' Peter asked.

DeLuca opened up the palms of his hands and put his head on one side in a gesture which clearly indicated the inevitability of a parting of the ways between them if such an eventuality came to pass.

'OK. OK. I'll see what I can do.' Peter said in a resigned tone, 'but if I come a cropper over this...'

Shortly after Peter left there was a knock on the door and DeLuca's daughter, Angela, walked in. She was certainly very attractive. Of medium height she had a slim, lithe figure with curvaceous hips and swelling breasts. Her thick dark auburn hair cascaded down her shoulders framing her regular features, which, although a little heavy for some tastes, were in keeping with her large, dark eyes and boldness of gaze which already had the power to hypnotise men who she wished to influence. She looked at least twenty, except when she didn't get her way, when a petulant look would betray the fact that she had not long left childhood.

DeLuca looked lovingly at his daughter. He was strangely unaware of her beauty, having not yet caught up with her sudden maturity. Although he lived for his daughter, he was aware that he had spoilt her over the years and that she had inherited his headstrong nature. She had become increasingly demanding recently, and he regarded her with a mixture of pleasure and apprehension as she approached.

'Hello Dad. Was that Peter Garibaldi I saw leaving? What was he here for?'

'Never you mind. Now what do you want?'

'Who said I wanted anything?'

'You rarely come to see me these days unless it's to ask for something,' he said only half-jokingly.

'As a matter of fact I do want something.' On saying this, she sat on her father's knee and put her arms around him. DeLuca prepared to say no.

'Dad, I want to get married.'

DeLuca pushed her off his knee. 'Married? At your age? No. Absolutely not. I forbid it. You're not pregnant are you?' he said with alarm, as an obvious explanation for her disconcerting request occurred to him.

'No, of course not,' Angela replied impatiently.

'Well, you are far too young. Who is he anyway?'

'I am not too young. I will be eighteen next month, and I'm not telling you unless you cross your heart and hope to die that you will let me marry him.'

'But, Angela, my sweetheart,' he encouraged in a softer tone, 'you have your A-Levels coming up and then university. You have your whole life ahead of you. You are a beautiful girl. You will meet lots of men. You are just too young.'

'But I love him Dad. I can still do my exams. Please.'

DeLuca was a skilled negotiator and knew when he was on delicate ground. He decided to play for time. 'Look, we'll see. Bring the lad round. Let me meet him and then I will consider it.'

'You already know him,' she replied in an unusually bashful tone. 'It's Mark, your nephew.'

'You don't mean Cosimo's brat?' he said in disbelief.

'Don't say brat. He's nearly twenty and Uncle Cosimo is his step-dad, remember.'

'It doesn't matter that Cosimo adopted him. I forbade you to see any member of that family,' he said in a dark voice, the strangled fury behind it making even Angela, who was not easily intimidated, appear unsure of herself.

'Well I'm sorry,' she said defiantly, 'I think this feud with Uncle Cosimo is stupid. I love Mark, and nothing is going to keep us apart. I'll get married anyway, whether you like it or not.' At which point she burst into sobs of tears.

Angela had a good technique when it came to crying and DeLuca rarely withstood its siege for long. However, on this occasion his defences remained unbreached.

'I have been indulgent of you Angela,' he said firmly, 'too indulgent, I see now, but I expected you to respect me, at least in this one way. You know it was my decided wish that we have nothing to do with my brother or his family. He is no better than a tramp, your uncle. You have chosen to disobey me. Not just disobey me, but spit in my face. If you marry that boy I swear I will turn you out without a penny. Now go to your room.'

Angela, now seriously upset, fled the room, slamming the door behind her, leaving DeLuca staring into space, his fists clenched on the desk, his face a grimace of anger.

5

'I didn't realise that Glossy was made in Felton,' Joe said conversationally to Mrs Morgan as they drove past Purrfect Pet Foods, a large, modern complex of industrial units in the centre of the town.

'Glossy?' Mrs Morgan enquired crisply. Joe looked at her and decided that she bore a striking resemblance to the nurse in low budget movies where straitjackets and lobotomies feature prominently.

'My cat's favourite food,' he explained.

'Ah,' she replied, in a tone that suggested the nutritional requirements of feline companions were low on her list of priorities. 'It has been here for forty years. Keeps the town afloat. Here we are,' she continued, driving into a paved area in front of a two storey Edwardian brick house. 'Be careful not to bang the car door as you get out.'

The front door opened into a narrow, ill-lit hall. Mrs Morgan led the way up a flight of stairs and into her office. She hung her coat carefully on a hanger and then placed the hanger on a hook on the back of the door. Turning to Joe, she indicated that he should sit on a plain wooden chair facing a large oak desk. She opened an adjoining door and issued a brief instruction before returning to sit in a considerably more comfortable-looking chair on the opposite side of the desk.

A young woman came in and placed a buff file on the desk. She gave Joe what he interpreted to be a smile of sympathy and departed. Mrs Morgan picked up the file and withdrew a long vellum envelope.

'Now, Mr Landseer,' she said, adjusting her glasses to give Joe a stern look. 'Your aunt's last Will and Testament.'

'Hmm,' Joe said, clearing his throat.

Mrs Morgan gave him a quizzical look.

'I was just wondering if my mother shouldn't be here. Oh, and Gran was my great-aunt you know.' He felt a certain satisfaction in catching her out over this.

'I have represented Miss Chevanage for the last twenty years,' Mrs Morgan said stiffly. 'I think you can assume that I know the difference between an aunt and a great-aunt. As for your mother, she is fully appraised of the contents of the will. Shall I proceed? Miss Chevanage's estate principally consists of her house, the Waterhouse, and the contents thereof; its adjoining outbuildings, thirty-five acres of farmland which surrounds the property, and about eighty thousand pounds in cash and shares. She has left a small bequest to Mr Bramley, who I understand you know and the rest she has left to you.' She looked at Joe, waiting for his reaction.

'Me? Why me?' Joe said in astonishment.

Mrs Morgan gave Joe a look indicating that he might well ask.

'I thought Mum would get it.'

'Miss Chevanage was a woman who knew her own mind. She was obviously very fond of you and I understand your mother is well provided for.'

'Wow.'

'I should say that Miss Chevanage indicated to me that she hoped you would keep the property in the family. This influenced her decision as she thought it probable that your mother, living in Spain as she does, would sell. I believe she did at one stage consider putting a condition on the will stating that if you did not live at the Waterhouse for at least ten years the bequest would go to charity. However she thought better of this, something with which I agreed. In my opinion you should never try and influence people from beyond the grave. Nothing good comes of it. The estate is yours to do with as you wish.'

'How much does it all come to? The house was in pretty bad shape last time I was there, as I remember. Doesn't it need a new roof?'

'The house is in a poor state of repair. Barely habitable. I believe there is some subsidence and it is prone to flooding. I am not an expert, but I imagine you would need much more than your capital to fully restore it. Land values have gone up a lot recently though. As it stands, with the land, the estate would be valued for inheritance tax purposes in the region of seven hundred thousand pounds. You will need about forty thousand pounds to cover the death duties. My advice, for what it is worth, would be to sell. Houses with character are fetching a good price, but another major flood and the house may be beyond repair. In fact I already have a buyer who is interested. I could give you an introduction. There is one other problem. The animals.' She paused for effect.

'The animals?' Joe echoed politely.

'As you know, your great-aunt kept animals. Quite a few of them, in fact. They are still at the house, being cared for by Mr Bramley. This is only a temporary arrangement. If you wish, for a small fee, I could manage their disposal.'

Joe, who was now in a most genial mood, smiled beneficently. *What a nice, helpful woman* he thought. *What generosity of spirit.* 'You have a good place lined up for them?' he enquired.

'In a manner of speaking. If you are agreeable I will see they are collected on Thursday. It is quite a burden on Mr Bramley. Let me know if that is inconvenient.'

Joe gave her an equable smile.

'Good. Well, if that is all...?' she asked rhetorically, indicating that the interview was at an end. 'Let me know if I can be of any further assistance, with the sale for example.' She handed Joe a card and gave him what he presumed was an attempt at a friendly smile, although the requisite muscles were clearly out of practice.

'Could I have a look round the Waterhouse, do you think?'

Mrs Morgan delved into the folder and produced a set of keys. She looked into the folder again and brought out an envelope.

'There is one more thing. Your aunt left you a letter.' She handed over a white envelope. 'Now, if you will excuse me.'

'Blimey!' Joe said to himself as he clattered down the stairs, his good fortune sinking in. *This is a turn-up he thought. The Waterhouse. All mine. Good old Auntie.*

He rang Louise.

'The lot. She left me the lot,' he said excitedly. 'Seven hundred thousand smackeroos.'

'That's amazing. What great news.'

'I won't need to work again.'

'Not quite enough for that, I fear,' Louise said sardonically, 'but at least we can move to Islington.'

'Come up for the weekend. I need to stay here and sort out her stuff. We can stay at Cambelton Hall. Celebrate in style.'

'I'd love to Joe, but I've got that seminar this weekend, remember. I booked it weeks ago.'

'Boring. Come on. We've got to celebrate. Champagne. Caviar. Kendal mint cake.'

'We'll do something next weekend. Really splash out, and while I think about it, could you do me a favour?' Louise asked, softening her tone. 'It's Felicity's birthday on Sunday and I've forgotten to get her anything. Will you go and see her? She lives in Oakwood – that's just around the corner from you isn't it?'

Joe blanched. 'I don't think I'll have time,' he said evasively. 'I'm going to be terribly busy what with the animals to feed and papers to go through. You know how it is with funerals.'

Judging by the crisp snort that emanated from the earpiece, Louise clearly didn't.

'Don't be silly. Of course you'll have time. I know you don't particularly like Felicity, but it's been tough for her lately and she bought me that lovely scarf for my birthday. She's always good at remembering birthdays. It makes me feel guilty when I don't get her anything. Honestly, it won't take you a moment. Buy her a book, something sloppy and romantic. She likes that sort of stuff. Promise me you'll see her.'

'I'll visit her if I can,' Joe prevaricated.

'Promise me,' Louise insisted.

'Oh all right,' Joe replied reluctantly.

'Thanks, you're a sweetie. Anyway, got to go. Love you.'

Joe found a small cafe on the edge of the market place and weighed up the pro's and con's of his situation over a plate of fish and chips. On the one hand he had suddenly and unexpectedly inherited a significant sum of money. Definitely a pro. On the other hand he had to meet up with Felicity, something he regarded as akin to going for tea with Gollum. Joe knew this was unfair as Felicity didn't look a bit like Gollum – apart from the eyes, and maybe the lips – but since seeing the film he hadn't been able to get the idea out of his mind.

Also, at their last meeting, Felicity had tried to seduce him. Actually, sexually assault him was a better description he thought, as he recalled the event with a shudder. Felicity was a college friend of Louise's who taught French at a private school in a pretty market town in Rutland. She was quiet, plain and dreamy. She had come down to London on a school trip last November when Louise was in Milan. Joe had been delegated to entertain her. He took her to a small Italian restaurant in Bloomsbury, near the halls of residence where she was staying. The evening had been dominated by her description of her husband's recent infidelity. Also a teacher at Oakwood School, she had discovered him in the master bedroom of their new executive-style house, in a hard-to-explain position, with a sixth-former called Bethan who, it is safe to assume didn't look at all like Gollum. Not one to confuse vindictiveness with mercy she had the satisfaction of seeing her husband sacked and disgraced, but the experience had clearly left its mark. She drank steadily throughout the evening, although without obvious enjoyment. Afterwards she had lured him to her room, ostensibly to give him Louise's birthday present, whereupon she had proceeded to push him onto the bed and cover his face with wine-sodden kisses while trying to unzip his jeans. Pushing her away as gently as possible, Joe had pointed out the discrepancy between spending the evening castigating unfaithful husbands and then trying it on with her best friend's boyfriend. Felicity had promptly burst into tears, told him that she had always loved him and said that it was different because he and Louise were not married. Putting it down to post-traumatic stress disorder, he'd picked up the present, made his excuses and left.

They had not spoken since. Joe hadn't mentioned it to Louise, not wanting to spoil her friendship with Felicity. He also knew, that being a jealous type, whatever he said, Louise would think he was partly to blame; that he had led Felicity on somehow. Best to let the whole thing blow over, he'd decided. *Still, a promise is a promise*, he thought, and as he washed the last of the chips down with a second cup of tea he decided at the least he had to give her a ring.

'Felicity. Hi. It's me, Joe. I'm in Felton. Louise asked me to give you a call.'

'Joe. How lovely,' Felicity replied pleasantly, without any hint of embarrassment. 'What are you doing here?'

'Do you remember me telling you my great-aunt lived in Freasby? She's just died. I've come up to sort a few things out.'

'That's sad,' she said matter-of-factly. 'How long will you be here?'

'The weekend,' Joe said, not entirely truthfully, as he had decided to spend a week or so enjoying the countryside.

'Where are you staying?'

'My aunt's place,' Joe said, forestalling any offer of a bed in the executive home. 'I would call on you, but I don't have a car.'

'I tell you what,' Felicity said enthusiastically, 'I can come over on Sunday, after church. About eleven, OK?'

Joe recalled that shortly after her break-up Felicity had found God. He wondered whether a prior dose of evangelism would make her more or less emotionally challenged.

'That would be great,' he said blandly, giving her directions.

'I shall be expecting a birthday treat,' she said enigmatically before hanging up.

It was mid afternoon by the time Joe was dropped off by the taxi driver outside the church. He set off through the churchyard, over a stile and down a footpath that went through a twelve-acre pasture that was owned by his aunt. The meadow sloped downwards towards the river, and from the brow of the hill Joe could see the Waterhouse, set in its acre of garden, protected from the river and surrounding fields by an impenetrable thorn hedge, the white blossom of the blackthorn announcing the coming of spring. To the north of the property a graceful inner screen of white and crack willows, just coming into bud, swayed gently in the breeze. The Waterhouse, which was built on the bank of the river, had started out as a boathouse for his great-aunt's grandparents. A thatched three-bedroomed house constructed from the local ironstone had been built adjacent to the boathouse for an unmarried daughter. His aunt had moved in during the war when her parents died and she had been forced to sell their rather grand country house to pay their debts. The house was of simple design, resembling a children's drawing, with a sitting room, dining room and kitchen downstairs, and three bedrooms and a bathroom upstairs. It was separated from the river by a towpath which joined the footpath from Freasby. Adjacent to the house, built along the line of the river were a number of brick and stone barns. The garden, half of which was taken up with a stockyard and vegetable patch, was bisected by an arc-shaped pond, over which spanned a rickety wooden bridge. On the far side of the bridge, on a gentle upward slope, was a lawn, several flower beds and the remnants of a grass tennis court, which had long since fallen into disuse.

Joe walked into the garden through a wooden door set into the hedge and saw Walter Bramley in the garage.

'Hi Walter.' I thought I'd come and have a look around.'

'That's right lad. After all, I gather 'tis yours now.'

Walter spoke in a soft, slow drawl, which was native to East Leicestershire. Attractive to the ear, it was quite unlike the nasal twang of the West Midlands or the flat tones of East Anglia. An isolated dialect, it was now rarely heard in its full purity.

'How do you know?' Joe asked, surprised.

'Miss Chevanage told me some time ago.'

'She left you something too you know.'

'So I understand.'

Walter rested his two hands on a fork he was carrying and leant his weight forward, looking at the ground.

'What you be doing with the house then?'

'Sell it I suppose. I wouldn't know what to do with a place like this and the solicitor says it needs a lot of work. In any case I live in London. I couldn't get up here more than a few times a year.' Joe felt curiously defensive, although he didn't know why he should. It was the obvious thing to do.

37

'Oh I see.' Walter said in his enigmatic drawl, that Joe nonetheless felt carried more than a hint of disappointment.

'Do you think I shouldn't sell it?'

'Not for me to say, but there is the animals to consider.'

'Mrs Morgan has said she has found a good home for them.'

Walter snorted derisively.

'She said they would be well cared for.'

'They look after them right enough at the knackers.'

'I can't believe she meant that Walter. I'm sure she's found another farm for them.'

'Them's a collection of old crocks, 'cept Harry that is. Who'd want them?'

Joe, not being acquainted with the animals in question and having no idea of their market value even if he had been, was in no position to judge. 'Harry?' he asked, side-stepping the question.

Walter walked over to a pigsty. He leaned over the wall and made a curious snuffling noise. Joe joined him in time to see an enormous white pig with large black spots emerging from inside the shed. It came up to Walter, who fondled its snout. Walter then picked up a bucket containing some vegetable peelings and turned them into the sty. Harry, for it was he, without further ado, got down to the serious business of keeping body and soul in harmony.

'Nice clean sty,' Joe observed, hoping to work his way back into Walter's good books.

'They be clean when they're looked after,' Walter observed sagely. 'Gloucestershire Old Spot. He'll win best pig at the Spring Fair, you mark my words.'

Joe sensed the reason for Walter's disapproval. He had a prize pig on his hands and didn't want to lose his chance of fame.

'You keep it Walter. Take it home.'

'No room for a pig. Margaret complains enough about the

pigeons. She wouldn't let me in the house with Harry. 'Sides, it's Miss Chevanage's pig. She always liked to have a go with a pig at the show. Harry here was her best for years. She said to me, "Walter, if there is one thing I would like to see another spring for, it would be to put the winning rosette on Harry." She loved that pig. Bred it and reared herself she did. She liked nothing better than a big, handsome Old Spot.' Walter looked mournfully at Harry who was making steady progress with his lunch. 'Still, if it's not to be.' He gave an exaggerated sigh.

Joe felt a large, pig-shaped cloud, darkening the horizon.

'Well. We'll see,' he said gloomily.

6

Fred Carter was in his office studying a map spread on a large, rough-hewn, oak desk, when there was a knock on the door and his farm manager, Phil Wager, walked in as he normally did at the end of the week. He was a man in his fifties, with weather-beaten features, a stooped gait from carrying too many bales of hay and eyes crinkled by years of looking into the sun. He and Carter had worked together for forty years and there was a bond of trust between them. Under Carter's supervision, he had run the farm, building it up from a fifty-acre smallholding to one of the largest and most profitable in East Leicestershire. They shared the same unsentimental view of the land as a raw material to be modelled by their skilled hands, irrespective of aesthetic or ethical values their one watchword being profitability. Conservative in all other matters, they believed in new technology and willingly embraced the latest farming methods, not least because of the subsidies that often went with them. The cathartic experience of near bankruptcy at the time of a swine fever epidemic in the 1970s when they were just starting out together, combined with the ever-present uncertainties of a farming life, had left them tough and uncompromising. When there were grants to grub up the hedgerows they were eager destroyers of the country's heritage, and now there were grants to restore hedges they were replanting them with the same cynical enthusiasm. They had even applied to be one of the GM testing sites, but Miss Chevenage had got wind of their plans and complained that it would affect her organic certification.

For some farmers the land is like an extension of their souls. The daily chores become so much a part of their nature that they feel indivisible from the animals, the fields and hedgerows, the ditches and copses, the barns and machinery that they know as well as the scars on their gnarled hands. This is the warp and weft of their world. To these people the vagaries of farming are like bodily ailments, a period of bad weather like a touch of bronchitis, a blight like an infected cut that will heal given time and patience. They grow old marking time by the height of the sapling oak in the corner of the five-acre meadow, or the silting of the pond by the old iron-stone workings. Only the land has permanence, and they want to be part of it until they come to rest within its eternal embrace, when they hope and expect their sons and daughters to stand, buffeted by the wind and sun, in their place. They are romantics in their gruff hearts, who view the land, not as a friend, for it is too unpredictable for that, but as an essence of life, a part of God. The land is not an adversary to be tamed, but an enigmatic force to respect and cajole. They are custodians not warriors. They are not sentimental. They need to live, and if that means draining a marsh or ploughing an old meadow they will do it, but reluctantly and with a sense of loss. A dying breed, they are the butt of jokes in agricultural schools for their lack of productivity and conservative ways. Carter and Wager were not of this sort. To them the land was inert and stubborn. A clay that had become hard and unmalleable; that needed large machines with strong jaws to expose the entrails where the profitable juices were to be found. Technology gave them the edge, and if the competition was too slow or hidebound to take advantage of the latest pesticide or new strain of wheat, more fool them.

'Everything OK?' Carter asked.

'For now. Some wet weather on its way though. Ground's soaked already. The International's playing up again. Hydraulics won't work properly. I think we should trade it in. Get another Ford with a front-end loader.'

'Go and speak to Wilsons in Braunstone. See what sort of deal you can get. We got it from there didn't we? Never been much use. Now just come and look at this.'

Wager walked over to the desk and looked at an Ordnance Survey map of the Freasby area. There was a red line drawn around the Waterhouse.

'See that field next to the village? I reckon we could get planning permission to put housing on that.'

'Do you think so?' Wager said doubtfully.

'I do think so. I've asked Jack Pearson along to discuss it. That'll be him now.'

Jack Pearson, a local builder, was a fit-looking, well-built man in his sixties with a ruddy face and an easy smile.

'Jack. How's things? I've just been explaining to Phil how we are going to make our millions.'

'I'd best be off Fred. Missus will have the dinner ready,' Wager said and left with a nod to Jack.

'Now, what did you say about those millions?' Jack said, as he tapped out a pipe into an ashtray and proceeded to refill it from a leather pouch, a movement that was so leisurely and practised it appeared as part of the natural rhythm of his hands. 'Mind you, in my experience it's a whole lot easier to talk about making money than the doing of it.'

'Right enough Jack. Right enough, but I think I have a real one here. Look,' Carter said eagerly, stabbing at the map with his finger. 'Here is Chevanage's place with its three fields: two away from the village next to my land and one towards the village with the footpath through it. That field comes right up against the churchyard. It's practically in the village. Ripe, I reckon, for a grand estate of five-bed homes for all those city types with a hankering after a bit of fresh air'.

'I didn't see you as a developer Fred. No subsidies in that, you know.'

'No money in farming any more,' Fred said morosely. To tell you the truth, my heart's gone out of it. I wouldn't mind hanging up my boots if I could get a bit to retire on. Hand it over to David. This would just do nicely for me.' He indicated the map with a wave of his hand.

'How are you going to get planning permission to build outside the village boundary?' Jack asked.

Fred gave a conspiratorial wink.

'That's the beauty of it. It ain't outside the village.'

'Well, I'm no orienteer Fred, but it looks plain enough to me that the village stops here'. Jack pointed to where a clear boundary separated the last houses of the village from the twelve acre field that Fred was discussing.

'Let me share a little secret with you Jack. Keep it to yourself mind. It just so happens that I have a cousin who works in the planning office at Felton, and he tells me that when they came to draw up the envelope for Freasby they included Chevanage's place. Goodness knows why, but I've had a peek at the map myself and sure enough, that field is part of the village. Mark my words.'

'You might get it through the officers then, but the village won't like it,' Jack said, taking a ruminative draw on his pipe.'

'Some will, some won't. More houses means more people, which means more business for some, and the school wouldn't harm with a few more children in the playground. These villages are dying on their feet with all these incomers. They work in the city, shop in the city, send their kids to private school. Look at them pair of London lawyers at the

White House. You'd think that shit don't smell, the way they act. You remember what it was like when we was growing up Jack. Baker and two butchers in the village then. We all went to the school together, kids could play out without being run over…'

'Aye, them was the days Fred,' Jack said with only a hint of a wry smile, 'when you could buy a pint for a penny and still have change over.'

'You may laugh, but all change ain't progress.'

'Change hasn't done you any harm Fred. Your parents used to be tenants of the folk that owned this place and now look at you. Lord of the Manor.'

'It's hard work that done that. Hard bloody work. Kids today don't understand that. My David, he thinks it all comes easy. That's what I like about them Asians. They know how to work hard; you can say that for them. Like Singhy in the garage. Anyway, enough of that. What about it?'

'You'll have some opposition right enough. Mark my words. Councillor Jackson for one. He's dead against any developments in the villages.'

'That's where I thought you could give a hand. You're always telling me about the friends you've got in high places. Good Party man, successful businessman, secretary of Felton golf club, Rotary club – chairman of the planning committee is in the Rotary, isn't he? You've got the gift of the gab. I reckon you could smooth any wrinkles if you had a mind. You help me with planning permission and I'll give you ten percent of the profits. You can build the place too. That's the deal.'

'Twenty per cent and we might manage it,' Jack said with a smile. 'That'll give me some lubrication to work with. We can build a few low cost houses for local people and put a new roof on the village hall to soften up any resistance.'

'Twenty per cent. It's a deal then?'

On Jack's nod of assent they shook hands. 'Keep it quiet

until I've bought the place. These things have a habit of getting out. No bloody secrets in a village like this. Fancy a scotch to celebrate?'

'I wouldn't count your chickens if I were you. Many's a slip and all, though I will have a quick one to wet the whistle. How will you get the Waterhouse? I thought you and old Chevanage didn't see eye to eye.'

'She couldn't stand me, nor me her for that matter. You remember it was her family that owned this place. Back last century they owned a couple of thousand acres around here. Gradually lost it all. They were right snobs. Used to turn their noses up at my father and grandfather. Now look at me. I've got the last laugh. Chevanage couldn't stomach me. She thought I wasn't respectful enough, that I should know my place. In any case all that organic crap gets on my nerves. What's more, she wouldn't give me right of way to get to one of my fields. I have to go all the way round over the railway, an extra two miles there and back. She was a witch sometimes. No, you could say we didn't get on. She was a battler though, I'll give her that.'

'So, how will you get it?'

'It's all been left to the nephew. A London boy. I can't see him wanting to live out there. I'll offer him a good price for the house and land. He'll be glad to be shot of it. I've asked Morgan to soften him up, not that she could soften a blancmange. No, I reckon it's as good as a done deal, fingers crossed. One for the road?'

'No, I'd best be off. Let me know when you've bought the place and I'll start making a few phone calls.

'Grand. Good. Thanks for calling round. How's Margaret?'

'She's fine, and your family?'

'Humph! That wife of David's leads him a merry dance, but apart from that, OK I suppose. Let yourself out Jack. You know the way by now.'

As Jack left, Fred returned to his map. 'Sure beats lambing?' he said softly.

Later that evening, Mark DeLuca climbed up a nylon fire ladder lowered from Angela's window and clambered athletically into the second-floor bedroom. Tall, and strongly built, his dark curly hair framed a good-looking, open face. He laughed quietly as he fell in through the window, knocking over a lampstand.

'This is taking things to extremes a bit, isn't it?' That ladder didn't feel any too safe to me.'

'Shh,' Angela scolded. 'Dad's only downstairs.'

Mark grabbed Angela and kissing her, pushed her onto the bed.

'Stop it Mark. Be serious. What are we going to do?'

'Nothing. You are going to be as sweet as pie to your old man and get back in his favour. I told you it was rash telling him now. You should wait till you're eighteen. Then you can do what you like.'

'You don't know him. He goes stark staring mad when it comes to your dad. What happened between them anyway?'

Mark shrugged. ' Probably screwed your mum or something knowing Dad.'

'Don't,' Angela said. 'That's horrible. Anyway, Dad won't change. Not unless we force him too. He'll cut me off and then we'll be broke and miserable, and I don't think I'm cut out to be hard up. Sometimes I think he loves his pigeons more than he does me,' she said petulantly. 'Like that new one he's just bought. Rosso, what a stupid name.'

'I know,' Mark said brightly. 'Why don't you kidnap it, ask for a huge ransom and use the money to elope with me?'

He smiled playfully, sliding his hand up her thigh. She slapped his hand and then picked it up, kissing the end of each finger thoughtfully.

'You know Mark, I think you are a genius. That's a brilliant idea.'

'Now look Angela, I was only joking. Kidnapping is a serious offence. Prison sentences are handed out for that sort of thing. Men in blue with funny hats get involved.'

'Stop drivelling and listen. Do you love me?'

'Of course I do, but that isn't the point. Its no use me pining away while you spend ten years locked away at Her Majesty's pleasure.'

'Don't be ridiculous. Daddy would hardly send me to gaol for taking one of his pigeons, and in any case, I'm not going to be the one doing the pigeon-napping. You are.'

'Me?! Why me?'

'Because, apart from it being your idea and being so brave and brilliant at organising things, if you love me you should want to do it.'

'But your dad wouldn't think twice about shopping me to the authorities. It would bring a smile to his face and spring to his step. It would embarrass my dad at the same time as getting you out of my clutches.'

'Then you'll have to make sure you don't get caught,' she said breezily. 'It should be easy. I'll get the pigeon. Come to my room on Monday night. That's Dad's snooker night. We can work out a ransom note and take it from there. I will be able to keep track of developments from the inside.'

'There must be a simpler way to get round him,' Mark protested, but before he could express his forebodings any further he was distracted by a lingering kiss. He started to take his shoes off.

'You can't stay tonight,' Angela said firmly. 'With Dad all suspicious it would be too risky. It'll be OK on Monday night.' And with a final kiss she pushed him back out of the window.

7

Joe woke to the sounds of birds chirruping outside the window and the distant perfume of fried bacon coming from the kitchen of the bed-and-breakfast establishment where he had decided to stay the night, not feeling up to the chilly charms of the Waterhouse. Remembering his good fortune, he undertook his ablutions with a cheerful whistle and a flourish of his razor, revealing a man who felt that the sun was currently shining in his direction. True, there was the little matter of Harry the pig, who came to mind as he tucked with good heart into the bacon, eggs and two sausages arranged invitingly on his breakfast plate. However, he felt that this was indeed a minor difficulty for a man of his talents and new-found wealth.

Walter had offered to show him around his aunt's smallholding. The B&B was just off Main Street, close by Walter's' home. Walking along Main Street Joe was almost run over by a horse trotting briskly past. The rider, whom he thought he recognised as the woman sitting next to Fred Carter at the funeral, gave him an irritated look as if it was his fault there wasn't a proper pavement. In fact Joe could have sworn she almost ran into him deliberately. However, feeling in a forgiving mood, he called out his apologies expecting some contrition in return, but the woman trotted on without a backward glance.

Walter lived in a small brick house, that was in the middle of a terrace of similar residences, built in the nineteenth century for workers employed at a sand-and-gravel quarry which supplied the ballast for building the railway. The house had a new extension at the back for a kitchen and bathroom, but was otherwise unchanged from its original design.

Joe was greeted by Walter's wife, Margaret, a charitable looking lady of the same age as Walter, with a ready smile and a hospitable manner.

'Walter's out the back with his pigeons. Where else you might ask. Now, can I get you a cup of tea?'

'Thank you, that would be lovely,' Joe said politely.

He walked through the house into a small back yard, which was almost entirely taken up with a large wooden structure six feet high and set about two feet off the ground. It ran the length of the garden. Wooden steps led up into the loft through a door from which Walter could be heard moving about against the soft melody of cooing pigeons. Joe climbed the steps and peered in. Walter was dressed in overalls and wearing a mask. He was talking affectionately to a pigeon while looking intently into its eye with a magnifying eyepiece. Joe had known Walter since his childhood when he spent his summers with his aunt. He had spent many hours following him around the smallholding, helping him muck out the animals or sitting on the tractor mowing the hay. He remembered Walter as taciturn but kind, always prepared to show him farming jobs such as how to cut a hedge or milk a cow. In recent years Walter had become even more unforthcoming and occasionally irritable, the result of age and arthritis, and it was this image that was uppermost in Joe's mind. He smiled as he watched Walter gently stroke the pigeon, recognising the soft touch beneath his leathery skin.

Walter turned round and beckoned Joe towards him. He

took down his mask.

'It's all in the eyes,' he said removing the eyeglass. 'Here, take a look.'

Joe screwed the glass into his right eye and tried to aim it at the bird's head. He couldn't see a thing. 'Very interesting,' he said as enthusiastically as possible. 'Is this a male or a female?'

'Good question lad. You can't find the sex organs on pigeons too easy. The best way in my 'pinion is to take it's toe like this and bend it back. If it's a girl it goes like this, and if it's a boy it goes across the other way. This one is Dolores. Now you go back down and let Margaret make you a cup of tea while I finish off. I'll be down in a minute or two.'

'I'd forgotten you kept pigeons Walter,' Joe said conversationally as they left the house half an hour later.

'Aye. Thirty year a' more.'

'How many have you got?'

'Twenty-one at the moment.'

'Do you win much?'

'Now and again.' Walter was a man to whom words were like water in a desert. Not to be wasted.

They took the footpath through the twelve-acre meadow to the house. The field was being grazed by a dozen sheep. They gave Joe a mournful look and bleated.

'Are those my aunt's?'

'Aye. Lleyn. Welsh sheep. Hardy. They be your look out now though. Lambing soon too.'

This Joe considered to be bad news. Hard enough to turn your back on a dumb-looking sheep, never mind frisky little lambs with their endearing gaze and helpless cries. He studied the sheep anxiously, half-expecting little legs to start appearing at any moment.

'Just how many animals did my aunt have?'

'Well, there is the sheep – eleven ewes and a tup – the

milking cow, who has just had her calf, a horse and a donkey she got from the animal welfare people, the hens, a dozen or so ducks and geese, Harry you've met, and a goat. They mostly a bit old, like herself, 'cept Harry of course.'

'Do you look after them all on your own?' Joe asked in alarm as he realised he had inherited an old animals home.

'Mostly. There's a young lad from the village, Mark, who used to help out on a weekend, though he can't come too often these days since 'e got a job. Miss Chevanage did a bit. She was still quite sprightly up until a few days before she died with that stroke. She hoped you would take them on.'

Joe felt this was most unfair. *I like animals,* he thought, *no question about that,* but he just couldn't see them all fitting onto the lawn in Brixton. Anyway, Louise would have a fit. No, they definitely couldn't be accommodated in London and there was no way he was going to bury himself in the country. He had a career to think of. Not a very flourishing career admittedly, but one always had prospects. What future would there be as a farmer? A lifelong battle with muck and mud. No, they would have to take their chance with Mrs Morgan. He was sure his aunt couldn't really have expected him to take over the animals. Walter was making it up, putting pressure on him because of that wretched pig.

'I don't think I can do that Walter.' he said, politely, but firmly. 'Now tell me how much of this was my aunt's?'

Walter pointed out the three fields that comprised his aunt's smallholding. They occupied a triangle of land bounded by the village, the road to Heby, a village two miles towards Leicester; and the River Wreake. It was enough to be self-sufficient, but not for an income.

'She managed two of the fields as pasture and the third fodder,' Walter explained. 'Pasture be unimproved grassland.'

'What's improved grassland?' Joe asked.

'That be a ministry term for getting rid of all the old

51

grasses – the fescues, cocksfoot, timothy and the like – and reseeding it with ryegrass. Improved grassland grows quicker if you give it enough fertiliser, but the flowers can't grow. You should see this place in the summer,' he said, waving his hand at the meadow they were standing in. 'Full of flowers. Always changing. buttercups, daisies, orchids, trefoils, ladys bedstraw, black medick. Grand names they've got. Fifty different types I've counted. Beautiful it is. Whole of Leicestershire used to be like it. Not now. All gone. Look at Carter's.' He pointed out the neighbouring fields, which even in the winter looked a darker, more uniform green. 'He's lucky if he gets a dandelion; and he cuts it three times a year for silage. Birds can't nest. Improved grassland my backside,' he snorted finally.

Joe looked at Walter in amazement. He had never heard him say more than one or two sentences at a time, and here he was waxing lyrical about the English countryside.

They continued down the footpath and into the farmyard and garden. Walter pointed out the bantam hens which wandered freely around the smallholding; the geese, who were in a hissing mood; Trigger the horse, who was intimate with a sad-looking donkey; and finally a small barn where a brown-and-white cow was being suckled by its calf.

'This be Daisy,' Walter said, leaning over the door to the barn. 'Gives beautiful milk she does. Rich as it comes.'

'And I suppose Junior is called Buttercup,' Joe said sardonically .

'It were your aunt that did the naming,' Walter said stiffly, ' and she didn't get a chance with the little 'un.'

The calf, which was brown and about the size of a large dog, stopped suckling and came over, sticking his wet nose against Joe's hand, his huge eyes looking trustingly up at him.

'Brown Cow. I'll call him Brown Cow. How now, Brown Cow?' he said to the calf, and chuckled.'

'That's mighty original,' Walter said, clearly unimpressed at the christening skills of the Chevanage clan.

As they walked back towards the house, Joe caught a glint of red coming from one of the sheds.

'Is that where the tractor is kept?' he asked, trying not to sound too interested.

'And the Land Rover.'

The Land Rover, which looked as if it had seen service before the war, was green with an open back. However, Joe's interest was focused on the tractor, a red 1973 Massey Ferguson 135. It had always struck Joe that one of the few perks of being a farmer was that you spend much of your time playing with tractors. They made a throaty chugging noise, closely related in a male infant's psyche to the chuffing of steam engines. Their shape, dominated by the huge rear wheels, suggested latent power combined with myriad functions. Their wiring, bared to the world, meandered down complicated paths before disappearing, like underground rivers, behind metal hatchings into the bowels of the machine. Best of all they had numerous levers and buttons, which controlled any number of moving parts. As a child Joe had thought the mere act of climbing on and off them to be source of endless delight. He had always loved tractors, and now he owned one. Before he knew what he was doing he had climbed up onto the seat and turned the key. The engine leapt into life. He grinned wildly at Walter.

'How do you make it work?'

'Careful lad. They 'ain't toys.'

'Oh, come on Walter,' Joe pleaded.

Walter gave him some basic instructions and with a whoop Joe was off, careering at a steady ten miles an hour down the drive. As he reached the gate which led out of the farmyard towards the Heby road he turned, taking a wide sweep over a corner of the vegetable patch, scattering a few ducks and hens in his path and headed back towards the garage. With fifty yards to go he realised he had forgotten where the brake was. He took his foot off the accelerator but the tractor kept chugging slowly towards an inevitable collision with the Land Rover. In desperation he stamped on every pedal and pulled on every lever he could reach, but while this appeared to do interesting things to the front-end loader, it had no effect whatsoever on the forward motion of the machine. Just before the point of collision he wrenched the steering wheel around, once again scattering the same gaggle of hens that he had disturbed previously. A cock, decidedly put out by this interruption, flew onto Joe's shoulder and pecked him hard on his cheek.

'Ouch!' he exclaimed, flailing at the bird while at the same time shouting to Walter for help.

The east wall of the house loomed in front of him. Another jerk of the wheel brought only temporary respite as he was now heading towards the pond. The spirit of discretion having the edge over valour he leapt headfirst off the side of the tractor, landing in a bed of nettles, just as Walter calmly jumped onto the tractor and brought it to an immediate halt.

Joe got up, rubbing himself vigorously in a forlorn attempt to reduce the stinging pain on his arms and face. 'Damn, shit, damn, ouch,' he said shamefacedly.'

Walter tried unsuccessfully to keep a smile off his face. 'You all right lad? Gave yourself a nasty turn there I reckon,' he said sympathetically.

Joe smiled sheepishly.

'I think I need a few lessons.'

'Now if you're OK, I'd best be off for my lunch. If you don't mind giving Harry his feed.'

As Joe accompanied Walter part way back across the twelve-acre field, he heard bird song that touched a chord of joy. Without knowing why, he was filled with an inexpressible sense of delight.

'What's that Walter?'

Walter pointed upwards at a small bird rising up from the meadow, silhouetted against the blue sky. 'Tis a lark.'

'Hail to thee, blithe Spirit...' Joe recited, remembering a favourite poem from his childhood.

'Bird thou never wert, That from Heaven, or near it...' Walter responded.

'Pourest thy full heart in profuse strain of unpremeditated art. You taught me that Walter,' Joe said excitedly, recalling a summer's day over two decades ago when they had stood near this spot and Walter had recited the first verse of Shelley's poem, as a skylark had sung overhead.

'Aye, that I did. Be seeing you young sir. Mind you give Harry his bucket now.'

8

Joe didn't finish all the jobs until past nightfall, by which point he was exhausted. Considering that he had more than earned a pint of beer, he tucked a book into the pocket of his overcoat and set off for the village. He decided that the Agricultural Inn looked more authentic than the Fox and Hounds and had the additional merit of being closer to home.

Whereas the Fox and Hounds, built in the nineteenth Century, had been modernised with a slot machine, mock-Tudor decor, pub food and a range of lagers, the Agricultural was a relic from a lost era of slow habits and rustic charm. A pub since the fifteenth century, it had been owned by the Wright's for a hundred years. The latest scion of the family was Annie Wright, a lady in her eighth decade who, despite (or perhaps because of), a generous respect for the medicinal powers of her own product, notwithstanding a touch of arthritis, was in good health. The inn sold a home-made scrumpy cider, called Freasby Jack and a two types of bitter from a small brewery in Oakwood. The drinks were fetched from barrels in the cellar, pumps having yet to be installed. Neither the beer nor the cider was for the faint-hearted, the scrumpy in particular paying scant regard to the modern marketing of cider as a drink for the urban youth.

The pub consisted of a large, rectangular room, with a fireplace in the wall opposite the bar and a dartboard at the end furthest from the door. This was in constant use, the Agricultural having one of the strongest teams in East Leicestershire. Annie ran the pub as if it were her own living room, and it was furnished with several battered sofas and an eclectic collection of armchairs. She treated her customers as guests and could be charming, forming firm friendships. She did not however, subscribe to the view that the customer was always right. Holding strong if occasionally eccentric opinions on most issues of the day, she had an unfortunate tendency to refuse service to people to whom she took a dislike. This occasionally involved calling on her obedient, and very strong son Gerald, to eject those misguided enough to protest too vigorously. Over the years these had included a number of the population of Freasby, so that she was considerably less successful than her competitor. Indeed, if the beer had not been so good she might have struggled to make any sort of a living. Nonetheless the pub had a devoted band of followers including students and other occasional visitors from the city, who treasured its unique flavours.

Joe went to the bar and ordered a pint of beer. He noticed, sitting at the bar talking to an older man, the woman who had almost run him down with her horse. He smiled tentatively, hoping to overcome any awkwardness, but she returned his friendly gesture with a look of icy disdain and turned back to her companion. Joe went over to a vacant sofa and sat down. Looking around, he noticed a vaguely familiar and rather attractive woman of about his age talking with another woman also about the same age. She glanced up and caught his eye. He tried smiling again, and this time was rewarded with a friendly smile in return. He took a long drink of his beer. He loved English beer with it's rich variety and long ancestry, enjoying it's acquired taste, the result of many years induction. A minor connoisseur he was delighted to discover that this beer was finely brewed and perfectly kept. *The simple pleasures are the best,* he thought, settling back and taking his book out of his pocket. As he did so, an envelope fell onto the floor. He remembered his aunt's letter.

"My dear Joseph

By the time you read this I will have joined my beloved parents and you will have become the owner of the Waterhouse. I suspect that you will have been surprised by this gift and I have written this letter to explain myself.

I have always loved you my dear, and those summers when you came to visit brightened up my old age. However, I must say it was not my initial intention to leave you the farm. My over-riding wish was to see the animals well cared for after I had gone. I therefore intended leaving it to Walter, who has served me faithfully over the years with little reward. However, he refused. He has no children, and in any case, he said it was wrong that it should go out of the family. It was he that argued you should have it. He has always had a soft spot for you and was convinced that when you saw the place again you would come to love it as you did in your childhood.

I must say, I remain unconvinced. You are a Londoner now, with a London girl and a big career. You have been different the few times you have visited me in recent years; not interested in the land or the animals. By the way I don't like Louise. I know I shouldn't say this, but you are hardly in a position to tell me off. She lacks heart and is quite wrong for you. However, if you are determined, make an honest woman out of her and get married. Anyway, I told Walter he was being a hopeless romantic to expect you to change overnight, but he just shrugged his shoulders, as is his way. I did of course discuss this with your mother as she had a right to expect something, but she did not want the responsibility.

I do not wish to bind you beyond the grave. You must do with the Waterhouse what you will, though I would like you to remember that it is all that is left of our family estate, which once covered two thousand acres of this part of Leicestershire. I do however, have one request. If you do sell, find the animals a good home. Don't trust that woman Morgan. I only use her because her father was the family solicitor, but she also has no heart and would happily see my dears sent off to Purrfect Petfoods. Also, don't trust Carter. He has a silver tongue but no manners. His family were tenants of my grandparents and he would love to get his hands on the Waterhouse. Lastly, I have written down all the special needs of my animals and left the list in the kitchen dresser. Look after them well.

With all my love
Florence

Joe put down the letter and took a gulp of beer. He brushed away some moisture that had accumulated in his eyes and was reading the letter again, when he noticed that the woman with the nice smile was standing in front of him.

'Joe Landseer isn't it?' she said with a soft west-country burr, holding out her hand. 'I was sure I recognised you. I'm good at faces, but I couldn't remember your name at first. Alice Burton. Do you remember, we met once at a party, years ago in Cambridge?'

He suddenly recognised her and began to feel light-headed. Tongue-tied, his mouth hung open like a feeding trout. Realising this was embarrassing, he shook her hand and forced himself to speak.'

'My God,' he croaked. It wasn't quite what he had hoped for, but the best he could do in the circumstances. This, after all, was a woman he had met for one night ten years ago, fallen head over heels in love with and never seen again. 'Alice Burton. Well

I'll be blowed,' he continued, slowly recovering his composure if not his linguistic artistry. 'You've got a good memory. What on earth brings you here after all this time?'

She gave a soft, musical laugh. He recalled the pretty young woman with mischievous eyes and lively expression who had captivated him all those years ago.

'You make it sound as if I came here to find you,' she smiled. 'I'm keeping my friend company. Her boyfriend is playing darts against the pub team. How about you?'

'My aunt, has just died. Great-aunt actually. She lived in Freasby. I came up for the funeral.'

'Oh, I'm sorry.'

'We weren't that close. Or maybe we were. I don't know. I hadn't seen much of her recently. Won't you sit down? Would your friend like to come over?'

Alice went back to her friend, who shook her head. Alice returned with her drink. 'She thinks we should catch up on old times, although there isn't really much to catch up on is there?'

'Can I get you something?' Joe asked, gulping down the last of his beer.'

'Orange juice thanks, I'm driving.'

As Joe waited to be served he looked surreptitiously at Alice trying to remember the details of the evening. It was a post-finals party. He was staying with a friend from school, and Alice had come up from Bristol. They had hit it off immediately, talked all night about everything under the sun, finally falling asleep, fully clothed, in each other's arms. As he had fallen asleep he remembered feeling that this was it, this was the girl he wanted to be with. Then, when he had woken up, she had gone leaving only a note saying, *Thanks for the best evening of my life. Alice.* That was it. He had tried to find her, searched all over, but not a sign. Later he had found out that she had come to Cambridge to go to a May Ball with her boyfriend. He had never discovered where the boyfriend had been that night.

'This is amazing,' he said, putting the glasses down on the table and settling himself into the armchair. 'Fill me in on your life story.'

'Where do I start? You remember when we met I was in my first year at Bristol, doing biochemistry? Perhaps you don't. I finished my degree and then my mum got ill with breast cancer and I went home to Totnes to look after her. She died, which knocked me for six. I was messed up for a bit, lots of drink and drugs. Nothing heavy, mind you,' she added quickly. 'I coasted for a couple of years. Worked in Boots. Got engaged to an old boyfriend from school. Looked after Dad who couldn't really cope without Mum. Thinking back I suppose I had lost my confidence. I'd always had it easy – good at lessons, good at games, popular with everyone.. I was an only child, so I was spoiled silly I expect. I thought the world was made for me, and then Mum dying... It was such a huge shock. I can't even think of it now without wanting to cry. You haven't got a hanky have you?'

Joe handed over a large, fortunately clean, white handkerchief that he had found in one of his aunt's drawers. Alice took it and blew her nose, trying to hold back tears.

'Thanks. God I feel so stupid. You are almost a complete stranger and here I am baring my soul. You must be a good listener. Still, enough of me. Your turn.'

'You haven't finished yet,' Joe protested. 'Go on – dead-end job, about to be married to local hero.'

'OK. So then I woke up one morning feeling bored to death and caught the train to London without saying anything to anyone. Just left a note. Wasn't that terrible of me? But I know if I had tried to explain everything I wouldn't have had the courage to leave. Dad was furious of course. He's only just started speaking to me again. Still, he has got somebody else to look after him now so he's all right. It was Matthew I felt sorry for. I think he was pretty upset. Most of it was hurt pride mind you. We weren't right for each other and he knew it. We wouldn't have lasted more than a few years. Anyway. I signed on and worked as a volunteer for a green group.'

'I remember you were keen on the environment,' Joe interjected,

She nodded. 'I got a paying job with them after six months or so and that was fun for a while, but then I got the feeling that everybody was in it because it was fashionable, not because they really cared about things, so I started to get a bit disillusioned. It was pretty boring most of the time too, stuffing envelopes, going to endless meetings where people just seemed to talk to show off. So I went back to college and did a master's. Then my tutor got a job at Leicester Uni and invited me to do a PhD with him, so here I am.'

'What is your PhD on?'

'Pigeon fanciers lung,' she said chirpily. 'I've got another year to go.'

'I know about pigeons,' Joe said excitedly. 'At least, I know how to tell which is male and which is female. All to do with the feet.'

'You must come on one of my field trips,' she replied with a smile. 'Be my pigeon sexing expert.'

'Come to think of it, I read about that disease in the paper recently,' Joe said, recalling the article. 'It caught my eye because I thought I had it. Tiredness and lethargy. It's a sort of pneumonia, isn't it?'

'No. That's psittacosis. You are as likely to get that from lambs as pigeons. My disease is a type of allergic reaction to the bloom on pigeon feathers. It can be really quite nasty. It's related to a disease that farmers get from mouldy hay.'

'Could I get that?' Joe asked in alarm, recalling his afternoon cleaning the barns.

'Farmers lung? I doubt it,' she reassured him. 'You have to be exposed to hay all the time. And now it's definitely your turn.'

He gazed at her, adjusting his memory to the real person before him. He was sure her softly textured brown hair had been long then. Now it was cut short, shaped around her delicate ears and finely sculpted neck. She was still very attractive. Beautiful brown eyes, warm, make-up-free complexion. A smiling mouth with generous lips. He resisted the temptation to reach over and kiss her.

'Penny for your thoughts?' she asked.

'Do you believe in love at first sight?' he replied, surprising himself. He hadn't meant to say that.

She smiled thoughtfully. 'What made you ask that?'

'I don't know,' he said truthfully, but having asked he wanted to know the answer. 'Well, do you?'

'I don't know, she said cautiously. 'I suppose it's the sort of thing that if you haven't experienced it you can't be sure, whereas if you have you can, but then I don't know how you would tell the difference between the real thing and a counterfeit – where you go all wobbly over someone and it turns out he's a shit or into weird sex or something. I believe in lust, if that helps. There was this guy, the one I was meeting at Cambridge – great body, but he turned out to be completely boring. Really egocentric. What about you? Do you believe in love at first sight?'

Joe looked at her and smiled. The sense of confidence and mischief that he had remembered was still there, but the naivety that had accompanied it had been replaced with a hint of doubt.'

'It's in all the books, so it must be true,' he said, defusing the question.

'That's right, I remember you were a bookworm. As I recall you were passionate about Raymond Chandler. You told me he was the greatest post-war novelist or something along those lines. I read the Big Sleep because of you. I loved the way you got excited about a book.

'I'm not sure I'm passionate about anything these days,' he replied ruefully. 'I still think Chandler is pretty good though. Perhaps "the greatest post war novelist" was a bit over the top.'

'It's coming back. After we met I asked one of my friends who was doing English about your theory, and she said that he wasn't even the best thriller writer, that he got all his ideas from Dashiell Hammett,' she said challengingly,

'That was such a trendy thing to say,' Joe said scornfully. 'Typical English literature crap. First of all they think thrillers are too common a genre to be good literature, and then just to show off they quote some obscure writer who nobody has ever heard of. Not quite true in Hammett's case, but the principle holds. Hammett was an inspiration for Chandler, but Sam Spade isn't a patch on Philip Marlowe and the San Francisco of Hammett has none of the atmosphere of Chandler's Los Angeles.' Joe paused to catch his breath, and caught Alice looking at him with a sly smile.

'See, you can still get passionate about some things.'

'I remember you had just read *Silent Spring* and were passionate about saving the planet,' he said, retaliating.

'I still am. Right now I'm helping with a petition against a free-trade agreement with America which would mean genetically modified foods from all those big agri-business monopolies. Nobody can accuse me of not thinking big,' she said with a smile.

'But it's you lot who are doing all this stuff,' Joe said teasingly. 'It's not English graduates who invented Frankenstein foods.'

'I don't work on plant genetics,' she protested.

'But it's all the same thing. Mucking about with nature in the name of progress. It's always struck me that the apple in Milton's Paradise Lost was the same apple that struck Newton on the head. We took the wrong path back with the enlightenment and now look where we are heading. Fluorescent turnips.'

Joe finished his drink with a flourish, feeling pleased with himself. Alice was about to offer a vigorous retort when her friend tapped her on the shoulder. Alice looked up.

'Hi. Is the game over? This is Joe. Joe, Sophie.'

They shook hands.

'We're off,' Sophie said. 'Slob-face here,' she indicated her boyfriend, 'wants to get back for the football. Can you make your own way back OK?'

As they left, Alice looked at her watch. It was half past ten.

'I'd best be getting going soon,' she said to Joe. 'It's been great meeting you again, but you still haven't told me what you do. I don't even know if you're married or whether you have children.'

'I live with my partner, Louise, in East Clapham – well, Brixton really. She's an investment banker. I am – or was anyway – a journalist, I got sacked a few weeks ago, and no, we don't have children. My aunt left me her smallholding so I am wondering if I should give it all up and become a farmer.'

'That sounds wonderful. I'd love to have place like that – grow my own vegetables, have lots of hens and a pig. I love pigs. Is Louise the one you fell in love with at first sight?' she asked coyly.

'How about you?' he countered, avoiding the question. 'I can't imagine you are single.'

'My boyfriend Andrew, is a lecturer at the university. He is in Boston at the moment, looking at a job in Harvard. Now he *is* a geneticist, one of your Frankenstein creators. He wants me to go with him to America, but that would mean getting married. Apparently that makes it easier for me to get work. I'm not sure I'm up for that at the moment though.'

Annie called final rounds, although there didn't appear to be much urgency to it.

'I'd best be off,' Alice said, getting up.

'I'll come with you to the car.'

Her car was a blue Nissan. She unlocked the door and turned around to face Joe.

'Smart car,' he said appreciatively.

'My dad bought it for me as a sort of peace offering when I came to Leicester,' she explained.

'It's been a wonderful meeting you like this. Can I see you again? I'd like to show you around my aunt's place. I should be here for a week or two. I can introduce you to my friend Walter. He likes both pigs, and pigeons. You two would get on like a house on fire.'

'I'd love that,' she said, 'Give me your number and I will give you a call.'

'The house doesn't have a phone and I'm out of charge.'

'Oh. I'll drop round then. One day next week. What's it called?'

'The Waterhouse – it's hard to find though. I'll draw you a map.'

'Don't worry, I'll ask in the village.' She gave him a kiss on his cheek.

Joe, with a pang of disappointment, knew he would never see her again.

Alice turned the ignition key, but there was only a click. She tried twice again with the same result and then got out of the car.

'Damn,' she said irritably.

'I expect the carburettor is flooded,' Joe said, trying to be helpful. 'Leave it a minute or two and I am sure it will be all right.'

Although not mechanically minded, Joe remembered his father giving such sage and, as it turned out, accurate advice to his mother when, many years ago, she had similarly become frustrated at their car's failure to start. Ever since he had retained a touching belief that this was the answer to most malfunctions associated with motorised vehicles.

'It's electric,' Alice said absent-mindedly. 'How bloody stupid!'

'It was only a thought,' he said, feeling rather crestfallen.

'No. I'm sorry. It was me who was stupid. I left the lights on and now the battery is flat. Damn, damn, damn!'

Joe, his equlibrium restored, felt his spirits rise as he sensed an opportunity. 'Why don't you stay over at the Waterhouse? It's a bit basic but there is plenty of room. We can get the car fixed easily enough in the morning.'

Alice thought for a moment.

'I'd better not. I don't want to complicate things with Andrew. He's bound to find out and he always gets the wrong end of the stick.'

Joe was confident that Andrew's reaction would barely register on the Richter scale compared to Louise's response if she found out.

'I'll call the AA, or get a taxi,' Alice said, getting her phone out of her pocket.

'What a nuisance. No signal,' she sighed, glancing at the screen.

'I could try pushing I suppose,' he said reluctantly, not really in the mood with two pints of beer and three packets of crisps lining his stomach.

'It might work,' said Alice doubtfully. 'I am not sure electric cars respond to being pushed, but it would be great to try, if you don't mind.'

'Put it in gear when I say go,' he said, moving to the back of the car.

He got into a crouching position and started to push. Nothing happened. He tried pushing again, his feet slipping on the tarmac. Nothing. He walked up to the driver's side, opened the door and, leaning across Alice, released the handbrake.

'Sorry,' Alice said with a shamefaced grin.

'Don't give it another thought.'

Again he pushed, and this time the car moved forward slowly, gaining momentum as it headed down the slope towards the pub. Faster it went, until Joe was almost running. He gave a final shove, shouting, 'Go!' as he tripped over and fell heavily onto the road grazing his hand. The car jerked forward, but failed to start, gradually coming to a halt on the edge of the village green. Joe went up to it, picking the gravel out of his bleeding wound. He felt faintly sick. He leaned in through the car window.

'I don't think you pushed hard enough.'

'Well I did my best!'

'I didn't mean it like that. And you've hurt your hand,' Alice continued, poking it with her finger, causing him to wince. 'It looks really painful.'

'It is really painful,' he said sourly.

'No need to be mean. I did say I was sorry. Look, why don't we both try pushing? You can jump in when we get going.'

'We'll never push it up the hill.'

'Perhaps someone in the pub could help?'

'Please come and stay, Alice. I'll be the perfect gentleman, I promise.'

'I know you will.'

'Put it down to fate.'

'Oh all right,' she agreed, 'I give in. Whisk me away.'

9

When Joe awoke he was conscious of a heavy weight on his legs. He lifted his chin above the quilt and squinted towards the end of the bed. A large, furry mass that looked suspiciously like a giant rabbit greeted his view. Concluding that the beer in the Agricultural had been stronger than he thought, he rested his head back on the pillow, closed his eyes and took a few deep breaths. Then, extricating his feet from beneath its weight, he sat up to study the creature in greater detail. Closer inspection indubitably revealed a rabbit the size of a small dog. It lay at the end of the bed, nose twitching, chewing casually on one of Joe's socks. Joe reached for the document that his aunt had left detailing the fauna of the Waterhouse, which he had taken the precaution of having close at hand. Hercule the Belgian Giant Rabbit seemed to fit the bill. *"Hercule is a friendly rabbit,"* he read, *"who is five years old. He is toilet-trained, more or less, can use the cat flap and enjoys sleeping on the bed at night. Carrots are a treat. The only problem with Hercule is that he likes to play with Hans the Great Dane, a feeling that is not always reciprocated and occasionally results in a requirement for stitches"*. Hans it transpired was currently on compassionate leave with one of his aunt's friends.

'Good morning, Hercule,' Joe said, adopting a friendly tone.

Hercule was of a strong and silent disposition. With barely a glance in Joe's direction, he continued taking giant-rabbit-sized bites out of the sock.

Joe eased himself out of bed and looked out of the window. The sky was cloudless, and the elevation of the sun told him that the morning was well advanced. Alice was in the garden. Wearing a straw hat and a blue gardening smock, with a basket of eggs under her arm, she looked very much at home. She was chatting to Walter, who was digging up some carrots. Joe watched him alternately turning over the soil, then leaning on his fork. Two digs one lean seemed to be Walter's natural rhythm. Alice looked up and waved.

Joe got dressed. This involved a tug of war with Hercule and resulted in Joe descending the stairs with only one sock, a fact that was silently remarked upon by Alice as he entered the kitchen

'Hercule ate it,' Joe explained.

'Ah,' Alice replied.

She looked charming, he thought. The chill March wind had tousled her hair and flushed her cheeks, giving her a rustic appearance which suited her open expression and fine complexion.

'You look lovely,' Joe said, unable to hide his admiration. 'Quite the country girl.'

She blushed, heightening the colour of her cheeks and making her look even more attractive.

'I'm blushing aren't I?' she said touching her cheeks. 'I can't help it you know. I hate it. It makes me seem so girlish and yet the slightest thing and my cheeks light up like the Malin Head Lighthouse. Anyway, I should feel at home. My uncle had a place just like this in Chudleigh. I used to visit most weekends as a child. How you can think of selling it I have no idea. It's wonderful.'

'Aye, you tell him miss.' Walter said, his usually deadpan voice sounding almost enthusiastic.

'I see you've met Walter.'

'Walter was telling me about Harry.'

There's a surprise, Joe thought.

'Do you use the Natural or the Widowhood system?' Alice enquired.

'You know about pigeons then?' Walter asked in surprise

'She's a world expert on pigeon fancier's liver,' Joe said proudly.

'Lung,' Alice explained. 'Pigeon fancier's lung.'

'Oh yes,' Walter said in his slow, ruminative way, 'I know a few that's got that. Never had any trouble myself. I'm a Natural man,' he continued, 'although my friend Arthur who looks after DeLuca's pigeons just on t'other side of Felton, swears by Widowhood. Not to say I haven't got the match of him in prizes mind, not when you make allowance for the money they spend and the number of birds they keep. No, it's Natural for me right enough.'

Joe looked at Alice in admiration. A woman who could make Walter string several sentences together without having to wait for a row of potatoes to be dug in-between, clearly had special qualities.

'I'd like to come and visit your loft,' Alice said. 'I'm as interested in those fanciers who don't get disease as much as those who do.'

'It'd be a pleasure Miss.'

Joe, fearing that the conversation was taking a distinctly *psittaci*-orientated turn when his stomach was sending urgent requests for a full English breakfast, picked up the basket of eggs and carried them over to the Rayburn oven.

'Who's for eggs?' he asked with a flourish.

'You like 'em raw do you?' Walter asked slyly. ''Cause that's all you'll get unless you stoke up that oven.'

Joe felt the oven, which was stone cold. Alice suppressed a giggle. Joe, whose mouth had been watering at the thought of a good fry-up, felt aggrieved. Walter was clearly getting above himself, he thought. Showing off in front of Alice.

'Never mind,' Alice said kindly, noticing Joe's crestfallen look. We can at least make some tea with the electric kettle. Would you like a cup Walter?'

'No. I'd best be off. I just came down to get some carrots for the Sunday roast.'

Joe started salivating again at the idea of a Sunday roast, a meal he had rarely enjoyed in recent years, Louise being keen on brunch at weekends. Pancakes and orange juice. All very well, but not quite up to a leg of lamb with all the trimmings. He was roused from his gastronomic reverie by Walter pointing out a list of jobs that needed doing. It was a long list. Joe felt exhausted just looking at it. Country people, he decided, liked lists. Lists of animals, list of assets, and most of all, lists of jobs. Endless jobs, most of which seemed to involve shovelling shit.

'We did most of these yesterday,' Joe complained.

'That's the nature of farming my lad,' Walter said sanctimoniously.

He needs to brush up his diplomatic skills if he's to have any chance of keeping me here, Joe thought grumpily.

'It won't take long,' Alice said brightly, looking at the list. 'I'll give you a hand to get you going.'

'Walter, we've got a problem with Alice's car. It wouldn't start.'

'Never mind miss. I'll ask Mr Singh,' Walter replied. 'He doesn't mind doing the odd job on a Sunday and he can fix most things. It's been very nice to meet you. I won't shake hands with all the dirt on 'em. You come up when you've finished here and we'll see what can be done about the car.'

'What a gentleman,' Alice said, when Walter had trudged off. 'He's obviously keen that you keep the Waterhouse.'

'That's all very well,' Joe expostulated, 'but look at this list! A life time of jobs. Heavy jobs too. You don't need a degree to move horse dung from A to B. And what about all these diseases farmers get? I've been looking them up. Farmers lung, we've covered that; then there's leptospiro-something-or-other, tetanus, listeria, cowpox, not to mention being run over by your own tractor. You need danger money.'

'Don't be such a hypochondriacal couch potato.' Alice admonished him. 'It won't take a minute. Come on. Here's your tea.' And, pulling on a pair of boots, she opened the kitchen door and walked purposefully towards the cowshed. Joe followed in a desultory fashion. *Couch potato indeed,* he thought.

Alice was the type to lead by example, and by the time he arrived she had started pitch forking the bedding into a trailer by the side of the barn. She heaved the straw with a smooth, almost elegant motion. It made Joe feel strangely tired. It was curious, he thought, how repetitive activity by other people could have such a somnolent effect. He eyed with longing a moth-eaten hammock that was slung nearby.

'You know,' he said as Alice paused in her work, 'the old days had something to commend them. Just think, if I was my great-grandfather with his two thousand acres and lots of servants, I would be playing a supervisory role while you, or rather your great-grandmother, would be doing the actual work. I might even have been gracious enough to let you clean my boots afterwards. Come to think of it, I expect this hammock, which looks about the right period, was placed in just this position so that I could take a nap in the sun, while you brought over the cider and picnic lunch'. To illustrate his point, Joe slipped off his shoes for greater comfort and leapt athletically into the hammock, intending to take up a position of masterly languor. Unfortunately his calculations of the age of the hammock were not misplaced and as he settled into its folds, the material emitted a loud ripping sound. Slowly his bottom appeared from between a split in the canvas. Joe struggled to free himself, but only succeeded in settling further into the tear, his bottom getting ever closer to the ground. He was left in a curiously folded position with his head and feet poking out from either end of the top of the hammock and his backside peeking out below. His sock-less foot looked particularly forlorn. Rendered virtually immobile, he could do little more than wriggle.

Alice approached, fork in hand. 'Well master,' she said, a wicked smile on her face. 'Quite a pickle we have got ourselves into here.'

'Alice, my dear,' he supplicated. 'You wouldn't think of doing anything you might regret later, would you? Now, if you were to help me out of this less-than-dignified-position, I could see to it that you were let off milking duties for a whole week.'

Although the policy of attack as the best form of defence had it's champions, Joe, trapped in a position reminiscent of an insect in a Venus flytrap, might have been better advised to be more diplomatic. Unable to resist the temptation of such an inviting target Alice started to prod his bottom with her fork, causing the hammock to swing gently to and fro.

'Ouch,' Joe cried out in genuine discomfort. 'You sadist. OK, I plead for mercy.'

Alice put the fork down and giggled. Joe looked at her anxiously, not sure if she was going to help him or visit some new torment upon him. He feared the latter.

'You know, I have always wondered whether you gentry are ticklish like us mere peasants,' she said cheerfully, and proceeded to find out by running a piece of straw up and down his bare foot.

Joe was, unfortunately, very ticklish. He squirmed and howled, but to no avail. Alice moved up the hammock and started to tickle his stomach where it had become exposed by his gyrations, but here she over-reached herself. Joe managed to grab her arms, and with strength born of desperation, pulled her on top of him, gripping her tighter as she tried to free herself.

With a loud crash the hammock gave way and they tumbled to the ground ending up with her lying on top of him, her eyes smiling gaily into his. A kiss seemed unavoidable when a distant peal of church bells triggered a vague recollection in Joe's head. A recollection that rapidly coalesced into a feeling of doom as a shadow fell over them. Joe looked up and brusquely pushed Alice off his chest.

'Felicity! I'd forgotten you were coming. How nice to see you. Would you like a cup of tea? This is Alice. An old college chum.' He waved casually at Alice, who was lying spread-eagled on the ground, her clothes in a state of some disarray.

'You bastard, Landseer,' Felicity snarled. 'Out of Louise's sight for a minute and you're at it like rabbits. You men are all the same. You… you pimp. Some birthday present. I am sure Louise will be delighted to hear about this.' And giving Alice a look of contempt, she stalked off to her car.

'Felicity. Come back. It's not how it seems,' Joe called after her, but without turning around she got into the car and drove off, the tyres skidding as she went.

'Who was that?' Alice asked in a shocked voice.

'Felicity Cornish. One of Louise's friends. She teaches at Oakwood School. I forgot she was coming round to pick up a birthday present.'

'I suppose it did look rather suggestive. Still I'm not sure I like being looked at as if I was a fallen woman or something. People shouldn't jump to conclusions.'

'Louise will be up here within hours if I know her,' Joe said, the thought filling him with dread. 'She'll be all right,' he said without conviction, 'she knows that Felicity is a bit off the wall these days. I'm sorry I pushed you off. I didn't hurt you did I? It gave me quite a turn seeing Felicity standing there. Still, it was fun for a moment, wasn't it?' he asked hopefully.

'It was huge fun. I hope I didn't hurt you with the fork.'

'I should be OK, as long as I get my tetanus jabs in time.'

'I'd best be getting along.'

'I'll walk you to the village.'

'There's no need. After all, she said slyly, 'you've still got to work your way down Walter's list.'

'Oh yes, the list,' he replied unenthusiastically. 'When can I see you again?'

'I'm not sure. I've got a busy week.'

'I can come to Leicester. You can show me around.'

'You haven't got a car. Anyway, Andrew will be back soon.'

'We can't just not see each other again. Not after all these years. Can we?'

Alice looked at the ground, undecided. Then she smiled. 'OK. I'll find time to come and visit you. Help with the jobs. Wednesday perhaps.'

Joe gave her a hug and a kiss on the tip of her nose, which caused her to both smile and blush. She turned to walk up the footpath towards the village, and as she reached the stile that led into the field she turned and waved. Joe waved back, the pleasure of her company suppressing a pang of guilt at being attracted to another woman.

The phone call from Felicity came through on Louise's mobile just before lunch. She hadn't minded being interrupted during her meeting. It had given her an excuse to escape from a lecture on "You and Your Employees: How to Make Ying into Yang", which was about how to deal with non-productive staff. It consisted of a series of platitudes about value-added input, the need for criticism to be creative and the importance of channelling frustrations into positive energy. As far as Louise was concerned this was all mumbo jumbo. Her philosophy on make-weight staff was simple: get rid of them. Pronto. Her irritation at the lecturer's expensive advice, delivered with fluent certainty, was not helped by knowing from an acquaintance who worked for the same consultancy, that he had absolutely no experience of personnel management whatsoever.

While the interruption had been welcome, the content of the call she could have done without. As she listened to Felicity's tale of Joe's infidelity she felt the familiar sensation of her stomach viciously contracting that she recognised as an upsurge of her finely developed sense of jealous outrage. Not that she altogether believed Felicity's story. It crossed her mind that Felicity had tried to make a pass at Joe and had been rebuffed, but there could be no smoke without fire. Joe hadn't been his usual self recently. She had put it down to his sacking, but now she wondered if there wasn't a more commonplace explanation; that he was having an affair. It occurred to her that the whole legacy thing was just a ruse to get away for a few days of illicit sex. She rang Joe but got no reply. *He never has his damn phone on; bloody Luddite* she thought crossly. As she distractedly pecked her way through the buffet lunch she knew she wouldn't be able concentrate on the rest of the course, so after lunch she slipped away.

The meeting was being held in one of the functional hotels that cluster around Heathrow Airport, and within the hour she had circuited the north-western corner of the M25 and was driving north past Luton on the M1. Traffic was relatively light and she was able to drive largely unimpeded, until, climbing a steady incline on the approach to Watford Gap service station, she had to brake hard to avoid crashing into a blue Mondeo which pulled out into the third lane to overtake a pair of lorries. To add to her frustration, the car only inched past the lorries, barely going over the seventy-miles-per-hour speed limit. She flashed her lights, ruthlessly tailgating him, but this seemed to make him go slower rather than accelerate. Her rage, which had been soothed by the fast driving, suddenly boiled over and, as she accelerated past the Mondeo, she blared her horn, giving the driver, a balding middle-aged man, a furious glance.

This confirmed her view of Mondeo drivers as the epitome of cautious, suburban complacency. *He probably has as suitcase of lingerie samples in the boot,* she thought contemptuously. Joe, had he been there, for he liked to tease Louise, would have pointed out that there was little difference between her, who sold money, and her Mondeo driver, who sold goods. He would however, have got short shrift, as Louise recognised no such kinship, supporting the axiom that it is the people on the rung above who despise you the most.

Louise's irritation was soothed by the gratifying surge of power from the engine of her red Mazda RX-8 sports car, as she accelerated to ninety miles per hour. She was a woman who liked to be in control. She had never been drunk or taken drugs and rarely confided her feelings with either her friends or her lovers. At work she was friendly and could be charming, but always businesslike, betraying neither uncertainty nor sympathy. She knew the support staff thought her a cold fish, but her efficiency, intelligence and ambition, had gained the respect of her male peers and the admiration of her bosses. She was one of the few trainee brokers who had been fast-tracked. Growing up in a pinched home in a dingy corner of Dagenham, she had come to see the world as a hostile place. Her mother was the origin of this distrust. Louise's father, at least according to her mother, was a philanderer who had numerous affairs before walking out, leaving her to bring up Louise and her younger brother on a paltry income as a secretary in the car factory which dominated the borough. The bitterness that her mother had felt at this desertion had been instilled in her child, leaving an indelible stain. Her mother had married again, this time choosing someone who was safe and apparently dependable, but who turned out to be simply inadequate. Unable to hold down a job he had become chronically disabled with back pain, an ailment which Louise had always suspected was fictitious.

Louise had developed the tendency of categorising men as either bastards or no hopers. In her early life she had invariably chosen the former; a series of handsome shits who were attracted by her looks and air of confidence, but soon grew impatient with her intelligence and independent spirit. Sooner or later they indulged their belief in infidelity as a male prerogative. This experience sensitised Louise's jealous nature which surfaced at regular intervals, often in unregulated explosions of violent anger. Deciding she'd had enough of macho men Louise thought that she would try Joe. He was good looking, but didn't take himself as seriously as her previous boyfriends. She found him interesting and was amused by his line in self-deprecation. Most of all, he seemed to want to get to know her rather than display her. He humoured her jealous insecurities, teased her about her social climbing and was supportive of her career. While she wasn't sure that she loved him – she wasn't sure she could love anyone – she liked him more than anyone else she had ever met. She had even considered getting married to him. However his spineless response to losing his job had awoken a secret fear in her that he was a closet no-hoper. Now she wondered, as she drove up the M1, if he was a bastard as well.

Two hours later Louise swirled her car into the drive of the Waterhouse, spraying dust as it slid to a halt. Joe stopped cleaning out the pigsty and tentatively approached the car as Louise emerged. Even after a long drive she looked immaculate. Despite being preoccupied by the effort of formulating a reasonable explanation for Felicity's no doubt colourful description of the morning's events, he couldn't help but notice the way her tight-fitting red dress showed off her slim figure, exposing, as she climbed out of the car, her long legs to well above the knee. With a toss of her shoulder-length blonde hair, a characteristic habit when she was cross, she stood facing him, her nostrils slightly flared.

'Well, where is she?' she asked, her voice betraying a seething anger which had been festering during her drive north.

Like a rabbit caught in headlights, Joe momentarily lost concentration and started musing on the comparative merits of Alice and Louise. Louise was undoubtedly the sexier of the two he decided, and more sophisticated as well. However, for the first time he noticed a sharpness to her features; a suggestion of meanness exposed by her anger. He contrasted this with the air of innocence emanating from Alice's optimistic gaze.

'Are you going to just stare at me like one of your sheep or are you planning to say something?' Louise asked sharply, shaking Joe from his reverie.

'Who?' Joe enquired disingenuously.

'Don't give me "Who?",' Louise said scornfully. 'That slut you've been shagging.'

Joe winced. Matters were serious indeed when Louise, who had pretensions to gentility, lapsed into vulgarity. 'It wasn't how it seemed.'

' I should bloody well hope not.'

Joe tried to give her a kiss, but she backed away.

'That's right. Humiliate me with my friends and then expect you can make it all right with a kiss. Typical.'

Joe smiled nervously. Louise had a mercurial temper which even after three years of living together he hadn't really begun to fathom, let alone control. Sometimes minor irritants would send her into a rage, whereas on other occasions she would take major setbacks with stoic amusement. However he'd had occasion before to bemoan Louise's considerable capacity for jealousy. The slightest flirtation and his life was a misery for days. He had developed a number of stratagems to ameliorate these episodes, largely based on shows of affection. A surprise kiss, a small but tasteful present and, of course, flowers, although this reliable stand by had to be used sparingly. Despite considerable experience – for Joe with his regular features, brown curly hair and deep-set Mediterranean-blue eyes, was not without attraction to the opposite sex – it was not at all unusual for one of his attempts at reconciliation to misfire, leading to a prolonged extension of his discomfort.

'Look. Nothing happened. It was a misunderstanding. You know what Felicity is like. She is obsessed with infidelity. Come and see the house. You must be tired after the drive. I've got a bottle of wine in the fridge, and I'll fill you in on what's been happening. Would you like to see Harry the pig? He's quite a looker,'

Louise looked increasingly impatient. 'Don't try your wiles on me Joe Landseer. I am not sure if I'm staying yet. Tell me about this woman.'

'It's simple. I met her once at a party years ago. We met by chance in the pub last night. She works in Leicester. Her car wouldn't start so, doing the decent thing, I suggested she stay the night.'

'You mean to say she slept here last night?' Louise said incredulously.

'In the spare room.'

'I should bloody well hope so.'

'I could hardly let her walk home, could I?'

'And what about taxis? Don't they have such things in Leicestershire? You expect me to believe that this woman, who you claim to hardly know, was prepared to sleep in a strange house with a strange man when all she needed to do was call a cab?'

'Well, it's true,' he said defensively. 'There wasn't a phone signal. 'It was just a friendly gesture. Nothing happened, and when Felicity turned up I had just fallen over and Alice was helping me to get up.'

'That's not how Felicity described it. She said you were half undressed and fondling her breasts.'

Joe saw his opportunity. 'That's a complete lie,' he said forcefully. 'I was fully clothed, apart from only wearing one sock that is. Hercule ate the other one,' he added by way of explanation, 'and I certainly didn't fondle anything. Felicity is mad. She's malicious. She just wants everyone else to break up as well as her. You can't believe her instead of me.'

He could tell that Louise was softening. She suddenly burst into tears and Joe, on cue, went over and gave her a hug. This was cut short by her pushing him away, her nose wrinkling.

'Pooh, you smell horrible,' she said, wiping her eyes. She went to the car and re-merged dabbing her eyes with a tissue. 'I'm sorry I get so jealous, she said sniffling, 'but you've been acting strangely recently and imagine how I felt when Felicity rang up to tell me in intimate detail about how you were fooling around with this strange and apparently beautiful woman.' She looked at him and smiled bashfully. 'You do love me, don't you?'

'Of course I do.'

They kissed, at first tenderly and then more passionately. Joe felt a stirring in his loins. Louise giggled. 'Are you thinking what I'm thinking?'

'At least part of me is.'

'You'll have to take a shower first.'

'The water's cold,' Joe complained. 'It will dampen my ardour.'

'I insist,' Louise said. 'You smell like a farmyard. I promise to make it up to you,' she continued suggestively as they walked hand in hand towards the house.

Joe was woken by the sound of voices downstairs. He got dressed and went into the kitchen. Fred Carter was sitting at the table chatting to Louise.

'Joe, darling. This is Mr Carter, he wants to buy the Waterhouse.'

'Good afternoon Mr Landseer. I was just explaining to your good lady here that I saw Mrs Morgan in Felton yesterday and she mentioned that you might be interested in selling up. My land is next to Miss Chevanage's; yours now of course, and it'd make a nice job to take on her fields. Naturally I would keep them like she wanted, the meadow and all, and I would take good care of the animals. I know that would have been a concern to your aunt. Mrs Morgan plans to take them to Brady's, the knackers, but that won't do. I will make you a good offer.'

'How much?' Louise asked eagerly.

'For a quick sale I would give you ten percent more than, say, the average of four valuations. Seven hundred and fifty plus, I'd imagine. We could have it all sorted out in a couple of weeks if need be. That would let you get back to London.'

'Ten per cent more than the top valuation,' Louise said firmly.

Fred Carter looked at her with a slow smile. 'Ten per cent over the top price then,' he agreed.

'How do you suggest we proceed?' Louise asked before Joe could speak.

'If you are interested, get a few valuations and I'll start organising the paperwork. If we both use Morgan it will speed matters up.'

Louise looked at Joe, who shrugged his shoulders in reluctant agreement. He thought it was all moving too quickly and he didn't like dealing with Carter, but it seemed the obvious solution.

'It's a cinch with these yokels isn't it?' Louise said gloatingly when he had gone. 'I'll get Brian, my friend who works for Street and Porker, to give us a valuation. They are expensive at the best of times and he will add a few grand if I ask him nicely. Two weeks and we'll be rich. You can make an honest woman of me.' she continued playfully, 'and don't look so worried. I won't insist on a white wedding.'

That night, in the Agricultural, over a pint of beer, Walter was catching up with the news from his friend Arthur.

'It's the strangest thing Walter. You know that Rosso I told you about? Well, keep it to yourself, but it's definitely a wrong 'un, queer as a goose's bottom. I even did that trick with the toes you told me about and the bird it's trying to pair up with is a male all right.'

'Who you calling queer?' Annie, the proprietor of the tavern, asked as she emerged from the cellar steps carrying a pint of beer.

'I was just telling Walter 'ere about this pigeon that ain't' quite natural,' Arthur explained.

'I don't know what you mean by natural,' Annie replied. 'I had a couple of male ducks once who preferred each other's company to that of any female, and those wildlife programmes on the box are always telling us about critters that are gay. That's the word they like to use, isn't it? Nice word too.'

'Still, it ain't quite right is it?' Arthur replied. 'You can't make young uns if you're that way, and that's what it's all about. What do you think Walter?'

Walter took a drink of his beer and ruminated for a while. He had the reputation of being something of a sage in the village, and both Annie, Arthur and a tall man of about Walter's age with a sour-looking face and stooped gait waited for his opinion.

'Strikes me that some folks are born that way, in which case it must be natural. That's how I see it,' Walter opined.

'Aye, I reckon you're right,' Annie agreed. 'That's what my cousin says about her Jonathan in any case. He's a nice lad, though I know that Barbara is always worrying about diseases like that HIV thing, although they can treat it now by all accounts.'

'They deserve it if you ask me,' the tall man said.

'Well, no one did Bert, and you keep shut of that nonsense if you want any more of my beer,' Annie scolded him.

Bert shrugged his shoulders and moved further down the bar, although still within earshot of the other two.

'Anyway, what do you make of Rosso?' Arthur asked Walter.

'I've heard of it sure enough, but it be a rare business. That thing with the toes ain't foolproof you know.'

'It carries its head like a cock anyhow.' I don't know what the boss is going to do. Cost him fifty thousand quid that bird did.'

'The papers said nearly a hundred.'

'Aye, but I overheard him talking to that smooth lawyer of his and they did a deal with the guy they bought it off. Some sort of tax dodge. Keep all this to yourself mind, or I'll get into no end of trouble.'

'What do you want now Bert?' Walter asked the stooped man, who had suddenly appeared at Arthur's shoulder.

'Now't from you Bramley,' he replied curtly, and, putting his glass down on the bar, walked out of the pub.

'Bert's a bad-tempered old sod,' Arthur said.

'Gives me the creeps,' Walter agreed. 'He was just like that at school. A tell tale good-for-nothing. Now't changes does it? Thinking about it, he drinks in the Huntsman in Knessington. That's where Cosimo, your guv'nor's brother lives, isn't it?

'Cripes. I 'ope he didn't 'ear anything,' Arthur said anxiously. 'My big mouth.' And he emptied his glass with a deep draught. 'Better have another to shut me up,' he said with a wink. 'Your round I believe.'

10

Monday started disagreeably for Joe and deteriorated thereafter. The first problem was Louise. She arose at 6am in a thoroughly bad mood. Joe became aware of this when he was woken from a rather soothing dream, which involved being fanned by the ears of two giant rabbits while he watched Harry doing the washing-up, by a sharp dig in the ribs.

'Ouch,' he said irritably. 'That hurt.'

'You deserve it,' Louise replied ungraciously. 'I haven't slept a wink all night with you snoring in my ear. This is the most uncomfortable bed I have ever slept in. The whole place is damp and stinks of animals and old people. I don't know how you can stand it. The sooner we sell this pigsty the better.'

Joe, who was a man in touch with his feminine side, perceived that Louise was not taking well to rural life. This did not altogether surprise him. A relentlessly urban upbringing meant that her idea of a day in the country was a walk in Brockwell Park. Still, he had a dream to get back to, and with the merest murmur of a wish for a nice cup of tea before she went, Joe turned over and tried to get back to sleep. This occasioned a kick in the groin.

'Bloody hell,' he cried, jumping out of bed, 'that really did hurt. Didn't your mother tell you that is a delicate place for boys? Why are you so cross anyway?' he added, seeing her furious expression.

'Why the hell do you think I'm cross? Do you think it might be because I've had to come all the way up here when I should have been at an important seminar only for you to completely ignore me so you can play at being Old MacDonald? And now, when I've got to get up at this ungodly hour to go to work, you lie there like Sleeping Beauty expecting me to make you a cup of tea. You are so selfish. You expect me to do everything. Make you tea, sell your house, organise your life and earn us a living to boot. I'm sure you would have made that bimbo of yours a cup of tea.'

'What bimbo?' Joe said crossly. ' I told you it was nothing. When have I ever even looked at another woman?'

'What about Jennifer?'

'That was before we were going out,' Joe said incredulously.

'Only just. We'd already met. Anyway, you should be making *me* a cup of tea.' she finished lamely.

Joe, his dream now not even a distant memory, accepted defeat and went downstairs. As he was trying to stoke the stove there was a knock on the door. Walter stood silhouetted against the grey dawn, holding a newborn lamb in his arms. It gave a pathetic bleat.

'You got a bit of problem 'ere, lad.'

'What's that Walter?' Joe asked with a sinking feeling, 'and what are you doing up at this time in the morning?'

'I'm always up by five to make Margaret her breakfast. She was used to being up with her shift at Pet Foods and she can't break the 'abit.'

Louise appeared in the kitchen and went over to Walter.

'It's nice to know that some men look after their wives,' she said, giving Joe a significant look. 'I'm Louise, Joe's fiancée. It's kind of you to help Joe with the animals until we get the place sold. I expect he's said that shouldn't be too long now. What have you got there?' she asked as the lamb gave another bleat.

'The mother died lambing. I found her on my way here. We've got to get some milk into this one if she's going to have any chance.'

'Well, I'm sure Mary-Joe here will be an excellent foster mother,' she said, smiling sweetly at Joe. 'Now if you'll excuse me I've got to drive a hundred miles to earn some money.'

'What about your tea?' Joe asked.

'I'll get something on the way. Sorry to be so bitchy,' she said, softening and giving Joe a warm kiss. 'You know how I hate getting up early. It was sweet of you to make the tea. I'll give Brian a ring and ask him to come up tomorrow. If he can make it I'll take the day off and arrange to meet him here. I won't come up tonight, I've got an important meeting that will go on until late, but I'll aim to get to you by about nine. Be good.'

Joe, who felt somewhat awkward that Walter had found him with two different women on consecutive mornings, shrugged in a hapless, man-to-man sort of way. Walter smiled back enigmatically.

'What does one do with an orphaned lamb?' Joe asked.

'Must get it warm and dry to start. Been raining,' Walter replied, wrapping the lamb in a towel and placing it on the floor in front of the Rayburn. He then busied himself getting powdered milk and a feeding tube from the larder. 'It 'appens every so often. We'll find a foster mother, but meantime you need to feed her 'bout once an hour. Small amounts mind. I'll be back after I've sorted out the dead 'un.'

Joe looked at the lamb lying on the floor. She gave a forlorn bleat. Joe picked her up and cradled her in his arms. She gave off a sweet mixed scent of wet grass and dung. She was thin and shivering, her pink umbilicus hanging down from her belly. She barely appeared to be breathing. He couldn't believe that she could live. He tried to make her take some milk, but it just dribbled down her face and onto his arm. He sat down in a chair by the stove and rocked the lamb in his arms. He was still there, fast asleep, an hour later when Walter returned. The lamb was dead. They buried her silently in a corner of the tennis court, alongside a number of other graves, a testimony to the fondness of Joe's aunt for her animals. When the grave was covered in earth they stood respectfully for a moment, Walter with his head bowed. An Angelus tableau with an English backdrop of willows and thorn. A soft drizzle sent trickles of water down their faces.

Back in the kitchen, Walter busied himself making some porridge to warm them up while Joe sipped a cup of tea reflectively.

'You know, I think that is the first thing I have seen die,' Joe said. 'It makes you think, doesn't it? Puts it in perspective, all this struggling we do to get money and have careers. To get on in the world, make our mark and at the end of the day who cares?'

'You get used to death in the country,' Walter replied. 'It's harder when it's the bairns mind, be they human or animal.'

'I suppose they all go for meat in the end.'

'Aye, that be true enough. I like a good lamb chop, same as most folks, and I don't see now't wrong in that, but I don't like this fact'ry farming. That ain't right. They all be God's creatures. We should show them respect.'

'Have you seen anybody die Walter? Were you in the war?'

'Not quite that old young sir, although I did my National Service. Still there was plenty of death to be had at home. I helped bury two of my sisters with TB and my son died in my arms before 'e was one year old. Measles they said it were. No injections in them days. It's a marvel the NHS, whatever they say.'

'I'm sorry Walter. I never knew. Did you not want to have more children?'

'We tried, but nothing came of it. Still, we been blessed by good health and fifty years of a happy marriage, and not many can say that. My son be with God and we'll be buried up in Freasby churchyard with him soon enough. Now, that's enough of me,' he said briskly, 'Eat up your porridge and then I must be getting on.'

After Walter left, Joe started on his chores. First and foremost was feeding Harry, who was waiting impatiently in his sty. He grunted enthusiastically when Joe approached with two buckets laden with Walter's special prize winning diet, a mixture of proprietary feed and vegetable peelings. It was hard to stay sombre when confronted with a happy pig, and Joe was soon whistling to himself as he cleaned out the sty. Breakfast over, Harry gave a contented grunt and looked at Joe expectantly as he closed the gate.

'What?' Joe asked, conscious that Harry felt his duties were not completed.

Harry disappeared and returned pushing a football in front of him. Joe let him out of the sty and watched as Harry started dribbling the ball with his snout before pushing it at Joe's feet. Joe kicked it away, whereupon Harry ran after it, his bottom wobbling majestically. A ten-minute game of football ensued before Harry dribbled the ball back into his sty and disappeared inside for a rest.

By late morning Joe had finished his jobs and walked into the village for an early lunch in the Fox and Hounds. He had noticed on an Ordnance Survey map that a bridleway went west from the village and, turning towards the river, then joined up with the towpath that went past the Waterhouse. Keen to explore, Joe decided to take the long way round back to his house. Although the sky remained overcast the rain had stopped and he set off in good spirits, greeting the occasional villager with a cheery wave or an enthusiastic. 'Good afternoon.' Soon after leaving the pub, he passed the woman from the church riding her large horse, a bay mare. She didn't look at him and he was careful to cross to the other side of the street this time, but he couldn't help feeling it was a little odd. It crossed his mind that she was following him. Perhaps Carter had sent her to spy on him he thought for a moment, before dismissing the thought as ridiculous.

As he settled into his stride he took invigoratingly deep breaths of the moisture-laden air that had that fresh, washed scent that follows rain. He stopped occasionally by the hedgerow that lined the lane to examine the nascent hawthorn buds and admire the blackthorn blossom which was speckling the hedges in lacy white patterns. He identified an occasional sparrow darting past, often carrying pieces of twig, the mild early spring encouraging nest-building. For the most part the hedgerows had been decimated by the savagery of the mechanical trimmer, but there were occasional stretches where more sympathetic management had left the hedge to grow tall and thick. Here the wild, tangled branches of the hawthorn offered food and shelter for the dunnocks, robins and tits as they prepared to withstand the final frosts of the season.

Joe left the road at a stile and walked across a couple of paddocks before entering a large field, laid to grass, with a single spreading oak in the middle. Sauntering along, he was lost in a melee of thoughts about London, his career, Louise and Alice. Halfway across the field he stopped to take in the scenery and catch his breath. Looking around, he noticed a herd of twenty black cows inspecting him from a low ridge about one hundred yards away. Joe was fairly sanguine about cows. Gentle creatures he thought, fortunately unaware of their own strength. Bulls of course were a different matter. Bulls required handling with tact and discretion, preferably by someone else. If caught in a field full of bulls a cautious retreat was in order, whereas a herd of cows one could regard with equanimity and press on with a whistle on the lips and a spring in the step. It would therefore be an exaggeration to say that he broke into a jog as he continued down the path towards the next field. Indeed, so relaxed was Joe about the idea of cows that his pace didn't even double, at least until he realised that his shirt was disconcertingly dominated by the colour red although he recalled an article that claimed that cattle were colour blind. Getting out of breath, he stopped. This was ridiculous he thought, being chased by a herd of cows. Determined not to be intimidated, he turned to face them. With satisfaction he noted that the cows stopped as well. It was then that he made a curious observation. The cows didn't appear to have udders. What's more the leading animal suddenly started pawing the ground, accompanying this distinctive action with a loud snort. Curiously enough Joe had seen similar behaviour on a recent television documentary about bullfighting.

This he quickly recognised was the nub of the problem. The programme had been about bullfighting, not-cowfighting. These were not cows, but bulls. It did occur to him that they were more likely to be adolescents rather than the mature article, but academic musings on the number of bullocks that were equivalent in goring power to a fully fledged bull, gave him limited solace. He was reminded of a moment in a poem by D. H. Lawrence when the great romantic realised that the swallows he was observing swooping through the Tuscan dusk were in fact bats, an observation that Joe recalled made the poet's scalp tingle. Joe felt that right now he could teach D.H. a thing or two about scalp-tingling. Before he could murmur *Pipistrellus*, he was forced into action. The bulls had started to advance, initially with some reserve, but rapidly gathering pace. His only hope was the tree. He sprinted towards it stripping off his potentially provocative shirt as he ran; *no point in taking chances* he thought. The bulls were gaining ground. He could hear the pounding of their feet, he could smell their bodies, he imagined their hooves tearing into his soft flesh.

He visualised the headlines in the *Leicester Herald: Death in the Afternoon in Freasby*. With a final, panic-inspired effort, he flung himself at the trunk of the tree and grabbed at the lowest branch, pulling himself up and scrambling up a further three branches to safety. The bulls milled about the tree, snorting and pawing the ground, clearly disappointed that their victim had escaped.

Joe leant against the trunk of the tree, grasping an overhanging branch for support. The air burned his chest as he slowly recovered from the effort of his flight. He looked down and noted that he had somehow climbed to about twenty feet off the ground. This both amazed and disconcerted him. Joe was not good with heights. As a child the fascination with all things vertical evinced by several of his friends had escaped him. Tree-climbing in particular he regarded with distaste. He liked trees well enough from a terrestrial perspective, but, as he had remarked on more than one occasion when accused of being a sissy, if God had wanted us to climb trees, he would have put more time into the design of our tails. He was just wondering how long it took to die of exposure when he saw a rider on horseback approaching him from the direction of the village. A saviour was at hand. Relief flooded over him. He waved frantically, shouting loudly. As he did so, his foot slipped on the lichen-covered surface of the branch. He clutched wildly at an adjacent branch, but lost his hold and plummeted earthwards. It seemed as if all would be lost when his belt caught on a large nail firmly embedded in the trunk apparently to hold a now rotten rope swing. Joe came to a sudden halt, suspended in mid-air, his back to the trunk, his feet at the level of a bull's nose. His body swung about the axis of the nail, his legs and arms gyrating like a puppet's. The animals, disconcerted by the sound of his fall, ambled away as the horse and rider appeared under the canopy of the tree. Joe smiled bravely.

'Just trying to get a better view of the countryside,' he explained. 'Seem to have got a bit stuck. I wonder if you could be so kind as to give me a hand to get down? If it's not too much trouble of course. If you could just move your horse towards me I could get my feet on his back and then perhaps I could free myself. Sorry to be such a bother.'

He did his best to muster a smile, but the expression didn't get beyond a twitch of his lips as he realised that the rider was none other than the woman who had tried to run him down the day before yesterday. He had a horrible feeling that meeting like this was not a coincidence.

She took off her riding hat and, tousling her hair, looked at Joe with a sardonic smile.

'Joseph Landseer. You've got yourself into a right pickle, haven't you? I remember you were never very good at climbing trees. I've been following you. A few bullocks wouldn't have hurt you if you'd kept still. Now, what should I do with you?' she asked, half to herself.

This rescue, Joe observed, was not going according to plan. At least not his plan. Country life, so pleasant half an hour ago, was taking on a distinctly sinister hue. He eyed the riding crop she was holding with concern. She looked normal enough, he thought, as he studied her freckled, rounded face for signs of the inbreeding that might explain a need for remedial attention in the hinge department, but you can never tell.

'You don't remember me, do you? Jenny Savage ring any bells?'

Joe thought for a moment and then blushed deeply. 'No!' he said incredulously.

'And why not,' she asked. What do you think happened to me. Swallowed up by the earth?'

'Nan said you'd moved away,' he said. 'I did look for you.'

'You couldn't have looked very hard. We only moved to Heby. You humiliated me and then broke my heart,' she said, adopting a harsher tone that revealed a barely suppressed anger.

Joe couldn't think of anything to say. He was assailed by memories of his childhood.

'As I remember it, you said you would marry me when we grew up. I still have the ring you wove from the stalks of grass that day we spent on Robin-a-Tiptoe Hill. Have you come back to keep your promise, or had you forgotten all about me?'

To focus his attention on her question, she flicked him across his bare chest with the whip.

'Ouch,' he had occasion to say for the second time that day. *Who said women are the gentler sex?* he thought morosely.

'You ruined my life.' she said matter-of-factly.

'Jenny I'm really sorry about what happened. I couldn't find you when I came back the next year. Anyway I see you're married,' he said noticing the ring on her finger.

'In a manner of speaking,' she replied, 'Besides, it wasn't that I was talking about.'

Joe blushed again. He knew she was referring to one of the more embarrassing moments of his childhood; of his life so far, in fact. They had been eleven when they had gone together, in the middle of the summer holidays, to a barn to play 'doctors and nurses'. Jenny had taken off her panties and let him explore her pubescent sexuality. Then it was his turn. He had panicked. Refusing to take down his underpants, despite her vigorous attempts to undress him, it had ended with Joe bursting into tears and running off. Her father, a local farm labourer, had found out and confronted his aunt, who had packed him off to his parents. When he came back the next year, Jenny was gone.

'I can see you remember,' she said acidly.

'I'm sorry. It was a long time ago. We were just kids.'

'Kids, maybe, but that hasn't stopped me dreaming of revenge. I've been watching out for you ever since your aunt died. Now it looks as though you've been served up right where I want you.'

Joe, the memory of their last meeting vivid in his mind, was suddenly struck by the thought that Jenny was going to take her revenge by trying to undress him all over again. That, impaled on this nail, he was about to have his private parts humiliatingly exposed to the keen east wind that suddenly gusted across his bare chest. He involuntarily covered his crotch with his hands causing Jenny to snort with amusement.

'You worried I'm going to try and take your pants down aren't you. You should be so lucky. No I think I'll just leave you to swing for a while.' And putting her helmet back on, she quickly rounded up the bullocks and left them milling about under the tree before trotting away.

'Jenny!' Joe called after her pleadingly, but without turning around she just raised her whip and urged her horse into a canter.

Half an hour later, the bullocks having got bored and wandered away, Joe was able to extricate himself and jump to the ground, hurting his ankle in the process. He felt cold, wet and upset. *The sooner I get back to London the better,* he thought miserably, as he limped back to the Waterhouse.

11

After lunch on Monday, Alice drove out of Leicester towards Felton. She followed the directions she had been given by DeLuca, taking the road out of Felton towards Grentham. About a mile from the town she turned into a long, straight road. Half a mile down on the right, set up on the hill, was an impressive white house. She turned through a large iron gate, flanked by two stone pillars, surmounted by lions and drove slowly up the long, tree-lined drive. Close to the house, the drive opened out into a large circle with a lawn in the middle adorned by a bronze statue of a pigeon in flight. She parked the car and got out. As she did so, the light drizzle which had accompanied her from Leicester turned into heavy rain. With a glance at the increasingly dark sky, she ran to the entrance and hammered on a heavy brass knocker. An elderly man, dressed in a black suit answered and, explaining he was the butler, asked her to wait in the lobby. DeLuca appeared shortly afterwards.

'Miss Burton,' he said politely. 'You are from the university, I understand. Very important, a university education. I had to leave school at fourteen,' he confided, 'and look where I ended up.' He held out his hands to indicate the large lobby, with it's majestic curved staircase leading to a balcony that ran around the second floor, and chuckled at his joke.

'It's a lovely house,' Alice agreed, trying to sound enthusiastic.

'Seriously,' he continued sadly, 'I have always wished I had a proper education. I tell my daughter you get nowhere without qualifications these days, but does she listen? Clubs and boys, that's all she thinks of.' He gave a heartfelt sigh. 'She doesn't have a mother,' he explained, 'she died when Angela was young. I do my best, but she needs a mature female influence. Perhaps you could talk to her. Show her around the university.'

'I'd be very happy to Mr DeLuca.'

Angela, who had been looking over the balcony, curious to see who was visiting, came down the stairs.

'Angela, I would like you to meet Alice Burton. She's a sensible, unmarried woman with an education.'

'I'm not speaking to you,' Angela said huffily.

'You come here,' DeLuca demanded as she flounced out towards the gym, slamming the door shut behind her.

'Kids,' DeLuca said resignedly.

He led Alice into a large drawing room that looked rarely used, although a log fire burned in the grate, giving off some welcome warmth.

'Sit down young lady. Can I get you anything? A cup of coffee? Sims does excellent coffee.'

Alice smiled. She decided she liked DeLuca, even though her supervisor Dr Callum had hinted that he had a reputation as a bit of a rogue. In any case, she had to be nice to him, as the money he had given the university was paying her salary.

'It was very generous of you to give Dr Callum the grant for the research. He told me you have got pigeon fancier's lung.'

'That is true,' Mr DeLuca said sadly. 'And now I can't work with the pigeons. I used to love being with them. So friendly. Each one a character, and now I have to leave it all to my loft manager, Arthur. A good man, but it is not the same. I hope my money can find a cure for this disease. I find that you doctors are good at the diagnosis but not so good at the cure, eh? Now I understand you want some blood from me and a few of my pigeons to use as guinea pigs. Is that correct?'

'That would be very kind. Many fanciers have antibodies against pigeons, or rather the antigens on their feathers, but only a few get the disease. Dr Callum thinks it might be a subtype of the antibody that is important, and to test that we need blood from fanciers with the disease and ideally the pigeons which they train. That way, we can work out if different pigeons have different antigens.'

At this point DeLuca held up his hands in protest. 'Alice, my dear, I like your enthusiasm, but I can't understand a word you are saying. You are welcome to my blood and I will go and ask Arthur to look out four pigeons for you who are past their prime. Shall I ask him to leave them by the car? I trust you to look after them. They have given good service.'

Alice prepared her needle and syringe and expertly took a sample of blood from a vein in DeLuca's arm.

'You have a very gentle technique with that needle my dear,' DeLuca said, buttoning up his sleeve. 'Not like those butchers at the hospital,' he added ruefully. 'They always leave a most terrible bruise. It has been delightful meeting such a charming lady, and if perhaps you could advise my daughter I would be most grateful. Please do come again. Now I must leave you. Business never stops. Do make yourself comfortable by the fire for five minutes with your coffee. Sims will let you know when the birds are ready.'

Arthur was cleaning the cages in the breeding loft while the birds were out exercising. DeLuca had two lofts: a large, state-of-the-art affair for his 120 racing pigeons, and a smaller one for his thirty breeding birds which also housed injured pigeons and those nearing retirement. Arthur worked steadily in a long-practised fashion, humming tunelessly and worrying about his eyesight. He had cataracts and in a poor light had great difficulty seeing. He had been afraid that it was something more serious and had put off going to the doctor for as long as possible. Finally his wife and daughter had ganged up on him and forced him to go, but now he had to wait over twelve months for an operation. *A bloody disgrace,* he thought to himself. He had paid his stamp all his life and now, when he needed help, he had to wait until he was nearly blind. What really got his goat was that the GP had told him he could get it done within the month if he wanted to go privately. 'Two thousand quid,' he muttered to himself, as he brushed the droppings into a bucket ready for the compost. For a ten-minute operation. He had heard you could get it done for a few pence in India. A lifelong socialist he regarded the surgeon, who he suspected deliberately kept his waiting list long to encourage his private practice, as a traitor to the people.

What really worried him was that DeLuca would find out and pension him off. The thought gave him a spasm of anxiety. He loved this job. He wouldn't know what to do if he retired. He thought of his assistant Derek, who was ambitious to take his place. He didn't trust Derek. He had trained him up from a teenager ten years ago when he had come on a government scheme. He had done his best to teach the lad, but he had never liked him. Didn't show either Arthur or the pigeons enough respect. Mind you, he had to admit that Derek had some talent, although he would never make a great trainer. Didn't have the patience for it. He liked experimenting too much as well. Even now he was pressing Arthur to try a new feed. *I bet he's in for a commission from the supplier,* Arthur thought suspiciously, venting his irritation by forcefully scraping his shovel against a piece of hardened dirt. No, he didn't trust Derek one bit. He was the sort who would stab his best friend in the back if it were to his advantage. What was pressing on Arthur's mind was the feeling that Derek knew about his eyesight. At any moment he expected him to tell DeLuca. *That whippersnapper is a viper in the nest* he thought. *One slip and I'll be on the scrap heap.*

As if in response to his thoughts a knock came at the door of the loft.

'Art,' he heard Derek say through the wooden door, which was secured from the inside, ' Mr DeLuca wants four has-beens for a bint from the university. Put them in a basket and I'll be back in a tick to pick them up.'

It was a constant source of irritation for Arthur that Derek insisted on calling him Art, an abbreviation that he hated. He'd been called Art the Fart at school because of a penchant for baked beans and had never quite got over it. Time and time again he had asked Derek not to call him that. He knew he did it just to wind him up. His irritation at Derek boiled over into a frustrated anger. He felt a spasm of pain in his chest; a tightness that made it difficult to breathe. He took some deep breaths to try and clear the pain, but this made him feel light-headed. He began to feel nauseous.

The birds were now coming into the loft, encouraged by the darkening sky. A flash of lightning was followed by a rumble of thunder. Arthur counted the seconds. Eight. The storm was getting closer. He picked up a four-pigeon basket and moved over towards where the retired pigeons were kept. The loft was split into three compartments. One section was for the valuable breeding birds, including Rosso. This was adjacent to a section for the retired and injured birds and at the other end of the loft was the compartment for the standard breeding birds. Arthur started selecting some of the pigeons. They were all old friends and he didn't like the idea of them going to the university to be used for experiments. He looked into the beady eyes of an unusually plumaged bird and remembered the day six years ago when she had won Arthur and De Luca their hundredth race together. He and his wife had shared a bottle of champagne.

'No, you can stay with me,' he said to the bird, stroking her head. His memories were interrupted by a loud knock on the door

'Have you got those birds yet?' Derek asked sharply.

'You can piss off out of here and wait till I'm ready,' Arthur retorted angrily.

'What?' Derek replied. 'I can't hear a thing with this wind.'

Arthur turned and gave a vigorous two-fingered salute to the door.

'Come on, you old bugger, I'm getting soaked out here,' Derek called out, banging impatiently on the door. 'Let me in.'

I hope he catches his death, Arthur thought grimly. The birds, spooked by the oncoming storm were getting increasingly fractious, flying around the loft cooing loudly. He was putting the fourth bird in the basket when the loft was momentarily filled with light as a bolt of lightning seared the sky. This was followed almost immediately by a thunderbolt, as loud as a sonic boom. The lights went out and the bird viciously pecked Arthur's hand, escaping to one of the beams of the loft. Derek was now banging incessantly at the door. Arthur reached for the pigeon, but in the darkness he could only make out a dim shape and failed to grasp the bird. His chest pain started getting worse. He couldn't get his breath. He started to panic. Feeling faint and sick he put the basket on the floor and loosened his overalls. The pain started to go down his left arm. He sat down heavily on the floor, gasping. Dimly he saw the door of the loft fly open and Derek come in, a furious expression on his face.

Derek hurried up to Arthur who was now collapsed on the floor. Even in the gloom Derek could see that he was in a bad way.

'Christ,' he said under his breath.

He saw the basket lying on the floor with the one empty compartment. A pigeon was pecking unconcernedly just by it. He stuffed the bird into the basket, closed the lid and picking up the basket ran towards the house and up to Alice, who was sheltering under the front portico. He dropped the basket at her feet. 'Can't stop' he shouted, 'bit of a crisis,' Alice wondered if she should stay to help, but deciding it must be something to do with the storm and none of her business, she put the pigeons in the car and drove back to the university.

DeLuca's establishment was in a state of commotion for the rest of the day. The ambulance arrived and the paramedics confirmed that Arthur had suffered a possible heart attack. It sped off, blue lights flashing, leaving the household in turmoil. Derek was dispatched to inform Arthur's wife, while Sims went to the Leicester University Hospital to monitor his progress. The confusion gave Angela plenty of opportunity, later in the afternoon, to enter the breeding loft, open Rosso's cage and put the pigeon in a basket. Taking care to put another bird in the cage to replace him, she then sneaked back to her room.

It was also not surprising that, shortly after nightfall, no one noticed the small, blue Ford van parked on the grass verge half a mile from the house. Or, for that matter, the two men who, on leaving the van, proceeded to climb through a gap in the hawthorn hedge that bordered DeLuca's estate. The first man was small and chubby. He wore a worn, but serviceable, green waterproof oiled jacket, sturdy workman's trousers and a pair of heavy boots. Once through the hedge he hesitated on the bank for a moment before jumping, with surprising athleticism, over a water-filled ditch. He then turned to a slim youth, dressed only in T-shirt, jeans and trainers, who was making ready to jump.

'Careful son, that bank ain't half slippy,' the older man advised.

The boy failed to take his father's advice and, losing his foothold at the moment of taking off, slid into the ditch, his arms and legs flailing in a desperate and hopeless attempt to avoid submersion. Initially only in water up to his knees, he rapidly sank into the silt and became stuck up to his thighs.

'Dad, help, it's quicksand. I'm drowning,' the boy shouted in fear.

'Shush,' the father hissed, 'you'll let the whole bloody parish know we're here. Give me your hand.'

Pulled out of the ditch, the boy lay on the bank and started to sniffle.

'I want to go home,' he said miserably. 'I'm soaked to the skin and I stink of shit.'

'If you'd worn proper boots like I told you, you wouldn't have slipped, you bloody fool.'

The teenager started crying in earnest. The father looked at him in exasperation.

'Don't blubber,' he ordered. 'Here's the keys. Go and wait in the van. I won't be long. And don't turn the engine on.'

Although it was too dark to see more than twenty paces in front of him, Bill Martin walked confidently along the edge of the field in the direction of the house. Night-time jaunts such as this were all in a day's work. He worked as a free-lance countryman, hedge-laying in the winter, sheep-shearing and dipping in the spring, haymaking in the summer and helping out with the hunt in the autumn, but this was weary and uncertain work. It also barely made ends meet, especially when he found himself with a wife and, in quick succession three children. He had then begun to supplement his income with some poaching, rustling, badger-baiting and the occasional cockfight. It soon became known within certain circles in Felton that if you wanted to organise some rural skullduggery, Bill was your man. He could turn his hand to most things, and if he couldn't do the job, he usually knew a man who could. He had certain rules. He didn't do violence to humans, at least not if he could help it, and being a church going man he didn't work on Sundays. He was known to the authorities, but as outside office hours there were only two police cars to cover all of East Leicestershire and they had to watch their petrol consumption, it was actually quite difficult to get caught. He had done a few jobs for Peter Garibaldi over the years and had not been surprised to receive a telephone call asking him to steal one of Mr DeLuca's pigeons. Being discreet, he didn't ask why Peter wanted to burgle his main client and, not being of an enquiring mind, he didn't wonder too much about it in any case. His son had been pestering him to come on one of his jobs and although he was only fourteen Bill thought this would be an easy one to start him off. He hoped the boy wasn't going to turn out to be a disappointment.

He had cased out DeLuca's estate the day before and went straight to the breeding loft. Putting on a pair of leather driving gloves he took out some wire cutters and disabled the alarm system. Then, slipping the Yale lock he went inside, switching on a small pencil torch. He used this to identify Rosso's cage, which he opened carefully placing the bird in a black cotton bag. He pulled the drawstring tight and slipped the bag into a hidden pocket in the lining of his coat. He then placed a white envelope inside the cage and retraced his steps to the road. The job was done.

12

A rattle of stones against the window alerted Angela to Mark's arrival. She opened the window and secured the fire ladder to the sill, watching as it tumbled down the wall. It was a foul night. Black as pitch, she could barely see Mark as he inched his way up towards her, his body swaying in the fierce wind that hurled showers of rain into the room. Finally he tumbled onto the floor and she shut the window against the storm.

'Perfect night for a kidnapping,' she said brightly.

Mark gave her a cool look.

'I am totally soaked,' he said teeth chattering, 'you can't see a thing out there and it's freezing. I almost drove my scooter into the ditch twice. I tell you, I am not kidnapping any pigeons tonight,' he finished in a decided tone.

'You should get your father to buy you a car instead of going around on that stupid scooter. I'm going to get a car as soon as I pass my test.'

'Dad can barely keep his van going, never mind buy me a car. We aren't all rich,' he finished irritably. 'Brr,' he said, with a spasm of shivering.

'Hmm. You are a bit wet, aren't you?' Angela agreed.

'And don't forget freezing. Why couldn't I come in through

the front door anyway? I thought Moneybags was off playing snooker.'

'He is, but Sims is still on duty guarding the fortress. Come on, get those clothes off and into the shower.'

After an extended bathe a more cheerful Mark emerged from the en-suite bathroom, naked except for a towel around his waist. He had a powerful, highly toned body and a muscular athleticism that made Angela look at him admiringly sensing a frisson of desire. She went up to him and gave him a lingering kiss, enjoying the feel of his hands as they moved up her legs under her skirt and caressed her bottom. Determined not to be distracted she drew away from him.

'We need to discuss tactics.'

'Angela,' Mark protested, 'I really think we should call this pigeon thing off. Try another night when the weather isn't so bad.'

'No,' Angela said firmly, 'Look. I've already got it.' She pulled out a basket from under the bed and cautiously opened the top to reveal a pigeon sitting quietly on some woodchips. 'It's simple. All you have to do is find a place to hide it. You could put it with your father's pigeons. Then if it did get found he would be blamed.'

'That reminds me,' Mark said. I overheard Dad talking to some old geezer from the village who said that your father had some sort of tax scam with this pigeon and he only paid half what he said he did for it.'

'Sounds just like him,' Angela said ruefully. 'We can use that to twist the knife if he gets difficult.'

'Now you are adding blackmail to kidnap. I sometimes worry about you Angela.'

'If you won't do it, I'm sure I can find someone who will help me,' Angela said teasingly.

'I suppose you mean that old perv of a solicitor.'

'He's not so old, and at least he showed some interest in

me when the only thing that got you excited was a game of football.'

'Angela,' Mark asked shyly, ' you never, you know... did anything with him, did you?'

'Of course not,' Angela replied, evading his gaze. 'You were my first,' she lied, 'you know that. I only wanted to make you feel jealous. It seemed to work, too,' she continued, taking his hand and putting it inside her blouse. He slipped the blouse over her shoulders kissing the top of her breasts. She undid her bra and allowed Mark to fondle her nipples as she unzipped her skirt and let it to drop to the floor. Then she lay back on the bed and watched as Mark peeled off her knickers. Opening her legs, she pulled him on top of her, at the same time loosening the towel around his waist and feeling for his erection.

Preoccupied as they were, it was perhaps not surprising that they failed to hear the commotion outside the door. Sims, thinking he had heard a burglar and noting the ladder going up to Angela's bedroom window, had called DeLuca back from the snooker club. DeLuca, armed with his shotgun and hearing alarming sounding noises coming from her room, burst in gun at the ready.

Angela screamed, pushing Mark away and grasping for her blouse. As Mark stood up the towel dropped to the floor revealing a pulsing and generously proportioned penis standing to attention. He tried to cover it with his hands.

'Hello, Mr DeLuca, I'm Mark, your nephew. We have met.' It looked for a moment if Mark would offer to shake hands, but he thought better of it.

It is in times of crisis that we reveal our true selves. Mark was a polite, well-brought up young man. More likely to follow than lead, he had an optimistic view of the world and gave people the benefit of the doubt expecting others to do likewise. Angela, like her father, was made of sterner stuff.

'How dare you come into my room?' she shouted angrily at her father. 'I told you to never, ever to come in, unless I gave you permission. Now please leave while I put on some clothes.'

DeLuca, momentarily taken aback by this verbal assault, looked for a moment as if he might comply, but then the sight of his nephew's now-drooping organ returned him to his sense of purpose. He felt an eruption of anger that fast approached volcanic proportions, as the scale of his daughter's disobedience merged with fury at the thought of her being deflowered virtually before his eyes.

'Get out,' he said to Mark. 'The way you came,' he added, as Mark headed towards the door, 'and you can leave your clothes here. As for you,' he said threateningly to his daughter, ' I will deal with you later.'

'Don't move,' Angela ordered Mark, who had stooped to pick up the towel and was making his way towards the window. 'You will not tell me who I can and cannot have in my room,' she said defiantly to her father. 'Who are you to order me around? You've never loved me. You love your pigeons more than me. And you're a crook with all your tax dodges. I hate you.'

DeLuca, his face puce with fury, cocked his gun and aimed it at Mark. 'Get out,' he bellowed uncontrollably. 'Get out or I'll shoot.'

Angela picked the pigeon out of the basket and threw it at her father. The pigeon flapped into his face and caused him to jerk the gun upwards. It went off with a loud crash, splattering the pigeon against the ceiling. Angela grabbed Mark's hand and pushed past her father, who, unbalanced by the shot, fell over, banging his head against a dressing table. Mark and Angela fled down the stairs, past the bemused butler and out of the house. They clambered onto Mark's scooter, hidden behind one of the trees, and sped down the drive. DeLuca, leaning out of Angela's bedroom window, sent them on their way with an agonised scream of anger and frustration which merged imperceptibly with the howling wind.

A mile from the house Mark stopped the scooter and turned to Angela. Although not a major asset in a crisis he was a solid performer once he had found his feet. Angela, in contrast, had been thrown into a state of near shock by the turn of events. Mark with his towel and Angela wearing only her thin cotton blouse were not dressed for a night out.

'What are we going to do?' she asked miserably.

'Put this towel around you,' he said kindly. 'The first thing is to get you somewhere warm, and soon. You'll catch your death of cold, and anyway, we'll get picked up if anybody sees us like this. I'll take you to Mum's.'

'That's the first place he'll look.'

'Perhaps I should take you back. He'll have calmed down by now.'

'I'm never going back,' she said fiercely, and then burst into uncontrollable sobbing.

'I know,' Mark said brightly. 'Let's go to that place where I used to help out at weekends. The old lady has just died so it should be empty. I know where the spare key is kept. Come on, it's not far.'

Fifteen minutes later they arrived at the Waterhouse. Mark went into one of the barns, but came out again a few minutes later, wearing some overalls but looking disappointed.

'I found this to wear, but the key's not there. Walter must have taken it.'

He looked at Angela with concern. She was shivering and her eyes were glazed and absent. He quickly scouted around the house trying the windows. Then he remembered that Walter had asked him to take a look at the window of Miss Chevanage's bedroom, which had a defective catch. Getting a ladder he placed it against the wall and climbed up. He was easily able to open the window. He went and got Angela and guided her up the ladder and into the bedroom.

'Are you OK?' he whispered. She nodded. 'Get warm. I'll go to Mum's and bring back some food and hot drinks. I won't be long.'

She nodded again, content to follow his commands. Mark climbed down the ladder and laid it down against the wall. He rode off to his mother's house in Freasby, where he was greeted by a worried parent and two-stern looking policemen.

Joe's day had ended with a power cut following a particularly spectacular peal of thunder. He had therefore opted for an early night. He slept fitfully, his dozing punctuated by images of women in jodhpurs approaching him with evil intent, wielding riding crops. Following a particularly vivid dream he went downstairs to make a mug of tea. After reading his book for half an hour he went back upstairs, a candle in his hand. As he entered his bedroom he was surprised to see, curled up under the quilt, the vague outline of a form which looked distinctly human in shape. For a moment he thought that it must be Hercule, his shape distorted by the candlelight, but as he came closer he discerned the head of a young woman sucking her thumb. He touched the side of her face. Her skin felt like marble. She started at his touch and sat up, looking at him with large, doleful eyes.

'Who are you?' she asked anxiously.

'I live here. Who are you? What's happened to you?'

She considered this for a moment and then shook her head.

'It's a long story. My boyfriend will be back soon. He will explain. I am very cold.'

She pulled the bedclothes tightly around her and started shivering uncontrollably. Joe noticed that her hair was soaking wet. He went and got a towel and handed it to her, but she seemed incapable of doing anything. Joe started to seriously worry about her. She continued to looked at him with a dull, unfocused expression.

'I am very cold,' she repeated.

Joe decided firm action was called for. Prising the bedclothes, which were now quite damp, away from her, he told her firmly to take off her blouse and proceeded to vigorously towel her down, averting his gaze as best he could to protect her modesty at the same time as getting her as dry as possible. Then he dressed her in a shirt, boxer shorts, a pullover and a pair of leggings that Louise had left and put her back to bed with as many layers of blankets as he could find. He went to make a fresh pot of tea putting two spoonfuls of sugar in the cup for good measure. By the time he came back, the colour was returning to her cheeks. He watched while she drank the tea waiting for her to explain what had happened, but after putting down the cup she snuggled under the bedclothes, and a few minutes later she had fallen asleep. Regarding this apparition as yet another example of how country folk were several standard deviations outside the norm, he shrugged his shoulders and went downstairs to spend the rest of the night on the sofa.

13

Joe awoke to the sound of a car driving up to the house. He noticed that Hercule was sitting on his chest, nose twitching inquisitively. He recalled the girl upstairs, and it occurred to him in passing that if this was Louise arriving, some sort of explanation for her presence would be required. This thought caused Joe to roll sharply off the sofa ejecting Hercule onto the floor in the process. The giant rabbit looked at Joe with an expression that suggested he was an advocate of the adage regarding the effects of haste on speed, before hopping off to look for a more amenable companion. Joe peered out of the window from behind the curtain. To his relief, and not without pleasure, he saw that it was Alice and not Louise alighting onto the path. His relief was however, temporary as he noticed the time was nearly 9am. Louise would arrive at any moment. Two strange women on the premises would not be any easier to explain than one. He put on his dressing gown and hurried into the kitchen just as Walter was opening the door to let Alice in. She looked charming Joe thought, her cheeks flushed with the cold, dressed casually in denim jeans and a green-and-white rugby shirt and carrying a wicker basket. His other female visitor was seated at the table, dressed fetchingly, if rather revealingly, in the shirt and boxer shorts he had given her last night, but without the leggings. Hercule was seated on her knee, accepting an occasional spoonful of porridge and looking pleased with himself.

He felt Walter deserved an explanation. Three different women in his kitchen on consecutive days was sending out the wrong message.

'I can explain,' he said. At which point he realised he couldn't.

'I didn't know you knew Angela,' Alice said tartly, giving Joe the sort of look that Humbert Humbert must have become accustomed to receiving.

'No need to explain.' Walter said, reassuringly. Angela here has been telling me all about it while I made breakfast. She's the talk of the whole village. Anyhow, it crossed my mind that young Mark would have brought her here.'

'Mark? Walter; care to enlighten us?' Joe asked quizzically.

'Ask the young lady.'

Joe turned towards her expectantly.

She put Hercule on the table and discreetly pulled the shirt around her thighs.

'What a cute rabbit. Could I have a cup of tea?' she asked, turning to Walter with a winning smile. She sipped her tea delicately, enjoying her audience.

'My father doesn't like my boyfriend Mark. He caught us together last night and completely lost his rag. He tried to shoot us. We ran away, but it was freezing and wet and I didn't have any clothes. Mark brought me here. He thought it was empty.

Thank you for getting me warm by the way,' she said to Joe with a coy smile. 'He rubbed me all over with a towel,' she explained to Alice.

'Quite the Good Samaritan,' Alice observed dryly

'She was becoming hypothermic,' Joe replied defensively. 'Are you sure that's all?' he asked suspiciously, turning back to Angela.

'What else could there be?' Angela replied evasively.

'And what happened to Mark?'

'He's been arrested,' Walter chipped in. Wouldn't tell the police where she was, so they took him to the station in Felton. Quite a to-do there was in the Agricultural about it. Freasby folk don't like anything to do with Felton authorities too well. Dates from the war. Felton was with Cromwell, you know.'

'No I didn't,' Joe replied. 'How do you two know each other?' he continued, nodding at Alice.

'Her father is the man I was visiting yesterday,' Alice replied. 'In fact the reason I came over was to find Walter. I need his advice about one of the pigeons I picked up. He looks sick.' She opened the top of the basket. 'At least, I think it's a he. I wondered if you could take a look at him. He's listless, won't eat and his coat has gone dull. I would take him back, but I feel it might be my fault, and anyway I think they might just put him down.'

Joe, momentarily disappointed that he was not the reason for Alice's visit, had a sudden spasm of anxiety. He looked at his watch. 'Ladies, gentleman and sick pigeon,' he said loudly. 'Much as I appreciate company, my girlfriend is expected at any moment and the presence of attractive young women on the premises may result in serious domestic discord. So if we could move along now, otherwise talking as we were of Cromwell, your host may well suffer the same fate as King Charles I.'

The ladies, gentleman and sick pigeon in question ignored him. Angela examined a torn nail while Alice and Walter studied the bird. Joe charitably decided that their failure to respond to his request was due, not so much to a lack of interest in his well-being, as a woeful ignorance of seventeenth-century English history.

'King Charles was killed you know. Head chopped off. Or hung, drawn and quartered, I'm not absolutely sure, but suffice to say he met a sticky end. You wouldn't like that to happen to me would you now?'

'You say DeLuca gave this pigeon to you?' Walter asked Alice curiously, closely examining a metal ring around its foot. 'Have you noticed there are no bars on its wings? That's very unusual you know.'

'He gave me this one and three others for my research. It was his keeper rather than Mr DeLuca himself who actually gave me the basket.'

Joe, deciding that actions speak louder than words, picked up a piece of string lying on the table and fashioned it into a noose. He then stood on a chair, placed the noose around his neck and, holding the free end high above his head, lolled out his tongue and started to make a loud gurgling noise. Walter and Alice glanced at him with disdain.

'If you ask me,' Alice said, 'I think it's pathetic to see a man in fear of his girlfriend. Its perfectly innocent Angela and I being here. I'm sure Louise wouldn't mind. I am looking forward to meeting her. It will give me a chance to explain about that misunderstanding on Sunday.'

Joe was about to go into some detail about Louise's unfortunate tendency to take a less-than-rational view of female competition, when one of the legs of the chair crumpled, sending him sprawling onto the floor, his knee colliding with the Rayburn with a loud thud. He hopped around the room for a minute or two his face contorted in agony, making sounds which bore witness to our close ancestry with the chimpanzee family. Recovering from the first spasm of pain, he looked around, ready to receive suitably sympathetic attentions from his companions. To his chagrin both women seemed oblivious to his distress. He sat down and made a deliberate show of examining his knee. Disappointingly there was only a minor graze to attest to his injury. He sat for a few moments, contemplating the hard-heartedness of women. He caught Alice giving him a pitying look and decided that she should enter the long list of women who were all mixed up about gender equality. On the one hand they claimed they wanted their men to be all sympathy and understanding, and on the other they wanted alpha males who didn't get pushed around. Well you can't have it both ways, he felt like telling her, but contented himself with sticking his thumbs in his ears and waggling his fingers. She smiled back sweetly, before returning to Walter.

'Was it Arthur who gave it to you?' Walter asked, ''Bout seventy with a bald head?'

'No, it was younger man. He seemed in a bit of rush. Why, is anything wrong?'

'Not wrong exactly. There isn't anything obvious, but you can't tell. Could be pigeon flu or psittacosis. Not much to be done. Best just to watch him for a couple of days. He could just be homesick. He'll probably perk up. You need to keep him isolated mind.'

'Isolated.' She thought for a moment. 'I suppose that means you can't look after him. And I can't take him back to the University animal facility.'

She looked at Joe, who was watching a large spider cross the floor. This reminded him of the tendency of certain female invertebrates to post-coitally devour their sexual partners. The preying mantis sprung to mind. He was on the point of drawing this connection between human and insect behaviour to Alice's attention when he noticed her standing in front of him.

'Joe, you wouldn't be a sweetie and look after this pigeon for a day or two, would you? Just until we see if it's going to be all right.'

Joe looked up. 'I'm not sure a pathetic sort of person like me could possibly take on such a heavy responsibility,' he said slyly.

'I'm sorry if I hurt your feelings,' she said, 'especially when you are such a sweet, generous, brave, handsome and charming man. And did you hurt your poor little knee then?' And she gave his knee a firm tweak with her hand. 'Was it this one?'

'Ssss!' he replied with a sharp intake of breath. 'Yes, it was this one.'

'Perhaps I should examine it.'

She pinched his skin firmly, causing him to wince.

'All right, All right, I'll look after it. What's one more animal amongst so many? Mind you, it's a costly business, looking after pigeons. Perhaps a kiss on my poor knee to make it better would help your pigeon to get that little extra care we all need when we are poorly?' He drew back his dressing gown to fully expose his afflicted joint.

Alice bent down and kissed his knee.

'Better?"

'Much. Another kiss and I would be well on the road to a full recovery.'

Alice bent her face down towards his knee for a second kiss, but as she did so Joe heard the sound of a car approaching and stood up suddenly, giving her a painful knock on the chin.

'Ouch, that hurt,' Alice said, in an aggrieved tone.

'Sorry. Really sorry, but it's her. Quick. Into the cellar.' And before the two women could protest, he had bundled them into the cellar, which was entered from the kitchen. He closed the door, urging them to be silent just as Louise walked in.

'God, the M1 is a pain. Nothing but roadworks. And people drive so bloody slowly. I thought I would never get here.' She went over and kissed Joe on the cheek. 'Make me a cup of coffee, will you?'

'You've met Walter before?' Joe asked rhetorically indicating Walter who was standing unnoticed behind the kitchen door.

'Of course, Mr Bramley, I didn't see you there.'

'Don't mind me Miss. I must be off anyhow,' Walter said, getting up to go.

'Don't go yet Walter,' Joe said, pushing him back into his

chair. 'I need your help with Harry. He didn't eat up quite as he should have yesterday.'

'I better go and 'ave a look then,' Walter said firmly, getting up and leaving.

'Is that Walter's car?' Louise asked.

'No, it was my aunt's,' Joe lied, thinking quickly. She'd leant it to someone in the village and they returned it last night.'

He made Louise a cup of coffee, and as he put it down on the table he noticed how desirable she looked. Not exactly dressed for milking duties, but none the worse for that. She wore an elegant, tight fitting, short grey woollen dress which outlined her ample breasts and showed off enough of her long, silk-coated legs to stimulate more than just his imagination. Her reddened lips pouted invitingly and her eyes, highlighted by a subtle touch of liner, smiled coquettishly. He moved close to her and brushed a lock of golden hair off her forehead. He then moved his arms behind her neck and undid the zip of her dress. Easing it off her shoulders, he let the dress slide to the floor. As he did so, he saw Alice's head poking out through the cellar door. He gestured her to go back. She gave him a look that Medusa would have proud of and withdrew.

'Let's go upstairs,' he suggested and he led Louise up to the bedroom, being careful to slip the bolt closed on the cellar door as he went past.

Joe was woken from a brief post-coital sleep by a sharp knocking sound. He glanced at Louise, who had a dreamy look on her face. He tried to extricate himself from her arms but she pulled him towards her.

'That was lovely. Let's do it again,' she said sleepily

'I think your estate agent friend has arrived. I'd better go down.'

'He can wait,' she protested as he crept out of bed and pulled on a pair of jeans and a shirt.

'Come back, I want more, more,' she cried out in mock desperation.

Joe, who couldn't restrain a smile on his face, hurried downstairs. As he feared the knocking sound came from the cellar. He unbolted the door and Alice, her face set in cold fury stalked past him, holding Angela's hand.

'I'm sorry,' he whispered helplessly, 'I couldn't get away.'

'How could you do that?' Alice said in a strangled voice and, picking up a bowl of congealed porridge, emptied it over his head. Then, dragging Angela in tow, she stalked out of the kitchen.

Joe followed, wiping the porridge out of his hair. He watched as Alice reversed at speed out of the drive, almost hitting a silver BMW that was coming the other way. A man got out of the other car.

'Women drivers, huh?' the man said in a smug yet ironic tone. This indicated that, despite being aware that such appellations were no longer politically correct, he also possessed an insight gained from *Iron John* that, in truth, only men could drive properly.

Joe gave him a neutral smile. 'Delivering post from the village,' he said by way of explanation. 'Always in a rush, even in the country.'

'Brian Seymour,' the man said, holding out his hand. 'I think we met at Julie's wedding.'

He glanced at the globs of porridge that still stuck to Joe's hair, but made no comment. Joe shook hands. He vaguely recollected this man as a surveyor who wore blazers and was keen on Grand Prix racing. He recalled Louise saying that he had once asked her to marry him. 'It's kind of you to help out. Louise is just coming down. Do you still go to the car races?'

Brian looked puzzled for a moment. 'Oh you mean Formula One. Not as much as I used to. Ball and chain you know.' I've got a wife and two kids now. Keeps me on the straight and narrow – talking of which, I spy a stunner.'

He brushed past Joe and walked over to Louise, who had appeared at the kitchen door. He gave her a distinctly over-friendly embrace. Joe felt a twinge of jealousy, which he suppressed as ridiculous. The man was clearly a half-wit. Not Louise's type at all. It was nonetheless with some pleasure that he watched him step back into some horse droppings and then shake a good portion of the dung over Louise's leg. She scowled, but took her irritation out on Joe.

'I thought you were going to get rid of these animals. When are they coming to take them away?'

'I'd forgotten about that,' Joe admitted, suddenly alarmed at the thought of their imminent departure. 'Thursday, I think.'

'About time.' Don't you just hate the country Brian? Come inside and wash your shoe in the sink. Would you like a cup of coffee?'

14

As DeLuca studied his reflection in the dressing-room mirror he was forced to admit to himself that he had been overly hasty in calling the police. He particularly regretted telling them that Mark had assaulted his daughter and then taken a shot at him, but he had to come up with some sort of explanation for the pigeon remains splattered over the ornate plaster mouldings. Still, it would have been better if he had delayed a moment or two to let his temper cool. These domestic matters were best sorted out privately, he thought ruefully. Now he had to go down to the police station in Felton and make a statement; awkward when he was also meant to be reporting a kidnapped pigeon.

He edged closer to the reproduction cheval mirror to examine his dyed, greased hair and make sure there wasn't any grey showing. His wife had purchased the mirror from one of the more expensive furniture shops in Leicester when they had first moved into the house. He would have preferred an antique, but his wife wanted everything to look unblemished to match the immaculate new house. She had been so proud, he remembered, showing off the Jacuzzi and the indoor swimming pool to her family and friends. He had loved the innocent way in which she had been unable to see their envy, carefully disguised behind barbed compliments, genuinely assuming that they were pleased for her sake that she had found a rich husband.

DeLuca was a dapper man, no more than five foot six, and still looked trim and fit despite his years. He didn't smoke, drank modestly and was rigorous about getting his heartbeat above 140 during his daily exercise session in the gym. *No*, he thought, looking at his reflection, *I intend to live a good few years yet. Not like that hopeless brother of mine.* He opened the wardrobe and looked through his array of bespoke, worsted wool suits. He had a weakness for expensive clothes. The soft touch of his silk shirts and elegant cut of his Jermyn Street jackets gave him a sense of poise and command. As he knotted his tie and adjusted the handkerchief in his top pocket, he heard a knock on the door and a quiet cough.

'Yes Sims?'

'Mr Fowler would like to see you sir. It seemed rather pressing. And Mr Garibaldi called. He said he would ring again shortly.'

Derek Fowler was indeed looking flustered. DeLuca tried to feign concern and waved him into his study.

'Yes Derek. What is the problem?'

'It's Rosso sir. He's gone.'

'What do you mean gone?'

'Gone sir. Vamoosed, and there was this note.'

Derek handed over a folded piece of paper. DeLuca opened it. A message was written in capitals cut from a newspaper: *GOT YOUR BIRD. HAND OVER TWENTY GRAND OR IT'S PIGEON PIE TIME.*

'It looks as if someone has kidnapped Rosso,' DeLuca observed coolly. 'Thank you Derek. I will deal with this. I expect the police will want to talk to you. Tell them all you know.'

'Yes sir. Thank you sir.'

'You can go now.'

'Yes sir.'

'Oh, and Derek.'

'Yes sir?'

'Apart from the police, keep this to yourself. Is that clear?'

'Yes sir.'

'Good.'

'Peter,' DeLuca said a few minutes later over the telephone. 'Did everything go according to plan?' I got the note, very artistic. Look, you will have to deal with the police and insurance people. I have got some business to attend to. A domestic matter. Use that inspector whose daughter we helped with a property last year – what was his name? – Rogers. He didn't seem the type to ask too many questions.'

When DeLuca arrived at the police station to give his statement he was ushered into a stuffy, overheated office. As he sat down at a desk, a man entered and took a seat opposite him. He was dressed in an ill-fitting suit and garish tie, which contrasted sharply with DeLuca's elegant attire. DeLuca smiled courteously.

'Inspector Harkins,' the man said, offering a hand for DeLuca to shake. 'I understand that you told my men the boy had attacked your daughter and then tried to shoot you.'

DeLuca looked at the officer across the table. A man of about forty with pudgy eyes and a thick neck.

'I was perhaps a little confused. It all happened in a blur. At my age, you know. The shock of seeing my daughter with this strange man. She is only seventeen. Such a thing should not be legal.'

'So he didn't attack your daughter?'

'He was naked and lying on top of her. What was I supposed to think? I am just an old man with old-fashioned values trying to bring up his child to be good girl. Her mother died when Angela was young. It has been difficult for me. Where is my daughter? Have you found her?' he asked with real anxiety.

'She left a message with the boy's mother. Your ex-sister-in-law I gather! I can't understand why you didn't recognise your nephew.'

'All I could see were his genitals most of the time. In any case I don't see my brother or his family. It was all such a shock.'

'Anyway it appears she is quite safe and staying with friends. I take it you don't wish to press charges?'

Mr DeLuca shook his head. 'Thank you for all your trouble officer. I am sorry for any difficulties I may have caused. A little something for the benevolent fund, perhaps? To show my appreciation for your help.'

As DeLuca was going down the steps outside the police station, he saw a battered ice-cream van, emblazoned with the name *DeLuca Ice Creams*, drawing up next to his Mercedes. He watched as his brother climbed out and started to walk up the steps. Cosimo was fifteen years younger, but didn't look it. His shoulders were hunched, and he shuffled rather than walked. His belly protruded over his loosely hitched trousers. He was wearing a brown smock, stained with ice cream, which, combined with his shock of thick white hair, made him look like an advert for one of his own products. As he got closer, DeLuca could see the blue veins criss-crossing his brother's purple nose belying his fondness for sweet cider. DeLuca compared this dissolute state with the freshly scrubbed teenager he had welcomed off the boat at Dover nearly forty years ago, an émigré from Italy hoping, with his brother's help, to make his fortune. Cosimo had worshipped his brother at first, always been eager to please, but it had all turned sour. They had never really got on, and when DeLuca wouldn't make him a partner Cosimo had become increasingly sullen. When he had sold off the ice-cream business to move into property he had given his brother a new van and they had gone their separate ways. It was the same van that had limped into the car park. De Luca watched in disgust as his brother took a final drag on a cigarette and chucked the stub casually onto the ground. For a moment it looked as if they would pass without speaking, but as Cosimo drew level he turned his head.

'You are a disgrace to the family, putting your nephew in prison,' he spat out in a thick Italian accent.'

'It was a police cell, although he belongs in jail. He's a paedo, that's what he is. My daughter's still a child. And don't talk to me about disgrace. Look at the state of you. You're like a tramp. No wonder your son can't keep his dick to himself. Like father, like son. You tell him to keep his fucking prick out of my house or the next time I swear I'll shoot it off.'

'Don't you blame my son. I bet he's not the first man she's spread her legs for. I'd put my van on it. Slut.'

DeLuca grabbed his brother by the collar, bringing him close. Cosimo, his lungs ruined by a lifetime of smoking, started to wheeze. DeLuca grimaced at his brother's breath, which smelt of cigarettes and yesterday's drink.

'You leave my Angela out of this, you bastard,' he whispered fiercely into his brother's face. 'I know you set me up over Rosso. Don't you worry. I'll get even.'

'Can't breathe. Let go,' Cosimo gasped desperately.

DeLuca pushed him away. He looked at his brother with contempt. 'You need to clean your teeth.' Straightening his tie, he walked down the steps towards his chauffeur-driven Mercedes, giving a passing kick to the bumper of the van.

'You don't fool me, Franco,' Cosimo shouted after him. 'I know how you got your fancy clothes and fancy car and fancy house. You're a crook. A lying, cheating crook. I've got a tale to tell, and one of these days, one of these days…' he screamed impotently, as the car drove smoothly away.

15

Joe left Louise to show Brian around the Waterhouse while he walked to the village to find Walter. He stopped off at the public telephone box and phoned Alice, but had to be content with leaving a message with Angela. He found Walter cleaning out the pigeon loft.

'Hi, Walter. I'm sorry about the mix-up earlier on. It's just that Louise can get a bit touchy sometimes.'

Walter carried on cleaning.

'I put the pigeon in one of the tea chests that Aunt had in the barn to attract owls. Seemed happy enough.'

Walter grunted non-committally. The dust made Joe cough. He backed away, not wishing to contract one of the many diseases that pigeons seemed to harbour.

'Walter do you remember a girl from the village called Jenny Savage? She'd be about my age.'

'Bob Savage's daughter? Best 'ave a word with Margaret.'

'She's in the kitchen, is she?' Joe asked in a conversational tone.

'And you'd best get them sheep in't afternoon. One of the gimmers be showin' signs.'

'Righto,' Joe said, wondering what on earth a gimmer was.

He retreated to the kitchen where Mrs Bramley was

preparing a meal. Joe felt at ease with Mrs Bramley, which wasn't always the case with her husband. A lifetime's fondness for her own cooking, which tended towards the traditional English mix of pies and pastries, had left her with a physique of generous proportions and a personality to match. She had a particular way with pastry that made it melt in your mouth.

'Are you staying for lunch?' she asked in a welcoming manner as Joe appeared in the doorway. It's chicken-and-mushroom pie.'

Joe was partial to all pies, but if he had to name his favourite, chicken and mushroom would get the vote. 'If it's not too much trouble, that would be lovely,' he replied enthusiastically.

'It would be a pleasure to have you. What about that girlfriend of yours?'

'She's taking a friend out to lunch. Can I do anything?'

'If you don't mind shelling those peas.'

Joe got a bowl and started shelling a large bag of peas. It was a rhythmical, soothing activity that reminded him of his summers at the Waterhouse where he would be sent out to pick the peas with Walter and later shell them at the kitchen table. He worked on the one-in-three principle where, for every two peas in the bowl, he would eat one. He liked their crisp texture and fresh taste even better raw. He bit one in half and chewed it thoughtfully

'Walter said that you knew Jenny Savage?' he asked casually.

'Little Jenny Savage. I was good friends with her mother, till they moved to Heby when Jenny was about twelve. I still see her mother from time to time at the WI, but she doesn't say much about Jenny these days. As I remember, you two were sweet on each other for a time,' she said with a faint smile.

'We were only children.'

'It's nothing to be ashamed of. She was a bonny child. Grew up a bit wild, I heard. There were rumours she'd got in with bad crowd in Leicester. It's a pity, her being such a butterfly growing up. The father was the problem. Nasty piece of work, especially when he was drunk. He took a strap to both her and her brother often enough by all accounts. Are you all right with those peas? Just put them into this pan. That's it. Next we knew, she was back here and married to David Carter, Fred Carter's son, and living up at the Manor House. She's got two children now. The first came a bit quick so people assumed that was why they tied the knot a bit hasty like. David always had 'is eye on her apparently, though neither of them seems too happy with life. There's stories about her carrying on, but then he drinks and I've seen her with a bruise on her cheek more than once, so what's right I don't know. I just know that she was as bright as a button and pretty as a marigold when you and she were friends, and now she's like a flower that's closed up for the night. It's sad when a life turns out like that. Anyway, what made you ask?'

'Oh, I just bumped into her, that's all. Can I lay the table?'

Replete after a splendid lunch, Joe walked back to the Waterhouse and found Louise sitting in the front room reading a book.

'How did it go?'

'Fine. He's going to give us a quote for eight hundred thousand. He'll get it in the post by Friday and then I'll ring that man – what's he called? – Carter. Now I must be off back to London.'

'I thought he was a bit of a dolt,' Joe said peevishly.

'Brian?' He's harmless enough. I rather like him in a way,'

'He seemed pretty horny with you. He tried to feel you up, and I didn't think you were exactly fighting him off.'

'I do believe you're a bit jealous,' Louise said, coming up and giving him a kiss on the nose.

'I'm not jealous. But he did want to marry you, didn't he? Did you and he ever… you know?'

'I don't mind you being jealous. Makes me think you care.

16

'What the fuck is that?' DeLuca asked Peter Garibaldi, pointing at a photograph on his desk.

Peter noticed that the late-afternoon sun shining through the French windows cast one side of DeLuca's face in shadow. He reminded Peter of one of the gangsters in the Billy Wilder film he had watched last night. This in turn reminded him of the intern in whose bed he had watched the film, and the rather tantalising way in which the cream that he dripped between her breasts had collected in her navel. He was about to continue his mental journey down her tanned torso, when he was brought rudely back to the present by the sight of DeLuca's expression of barely controlled fury. He was not a man who liked being kept waiting for answers.

'A photograph?' Peter said helpfully. 'I thought the insurance people would want some evidence that it was still alive, so I asked Bi…, my contact, to take a picture with today's paper, like they do in the movies. Looks quite good, don't you think?'

DeLuca gave Peter a sour look and then beckoned him to come round to his side of the desk. Peter started to feel uncomfortable. There was something about the measured way that DeLuca was acting that suggested the photograph idea hadn't gone down well. He edged around the desk, keeping his distance. DeLuca took a leaflet from a drawer and opened it to reveal a photograph of a pigeon. Above the bird was a headline. *Rosso Rummo. A Great Champion*.

'Come closer Peter, and tell me what you see?'

Although the request was benign, the tone was menacing and Peter reluctantly shuffled towards the two photographs and picked them up to get a better look. All pigeons looked alike to him. He knew from DeLuca's manner something must be wrong, but he had no idea what. He shrugged his shoulders.

'He looks a bit older in the second one?' he offered hopefully.

DeLuca grabbed Peter by his right wrist twisting it and making Peter gasp in pain.

'You bloody idiot! It's the wrong pigeon. Look. Most pigeons have wing bars. Rosso doesn't have wing bars. Now look at the two pictures. See. Rosso. No wing bars. Your bloody pigeon. Wing bars. You've kidnapped the wrong bastard bird.' He let go of Peter's wrist and walked over towards the window looking out at the gathering sunset.

Peter rubbed his wrist trying to suppress the many expletives that rose to his lips. He considered his options. *Flee and don't look back until you seen the light at the other end of the Mont Blanc Tunnel* seemed like the best one, except he feared that DeLuca would find him and do something unspeakable. His father had hinted about a dark side to DeLuca. He looked at the man's brooding presence silhouetted against the window. This kidnap thing was madness. He had warned DeLuca it would all go wrong.

There was a knock on the door and Sims entered carrying the *Leicester Herald*. He placed it silently on a side table and departed. DeLuca picked it up and read the front page. He then flung it in disgust at Peter. The headline read. *" Pigeon-Loving Property Tycoon Loses Two Birds in One Day."* This was followed by a story about his daughter running away, combined with the tale of his missing champion pigeon. A possible kidnapping was speculated upon and there was a reference to a mysterious ransom note.

'I thought I paid you to keep stories like this out of the newspapers,' DeLuca said broodingly, the edge of his anger having subsided. 'Vultures. I'll make sure whoever wrote that doesn't work again. How the hell did they find out about it anyway? Only you and I know what's going on, isn't that right?' He looked at Peter accusingly.

'Well, I didn't tell anyone. I hardly want publicity, do I? It must be someone from here. What really happened last night with Angela anyway?' Peter asked curiously.

'None of your business,' DeLuca said defensively.

'The point is,' Peter persisted, 'somebody must have switched the birds. So if we haven't got Rosso, who has?'

DeLuca thought for a moment, then the colour drained from his face and he sat down on the arm of the settee. He suddenly looked old and frail. 'Get Sims,' he whispered hoarsely.

'Sims,' he asked his butler when he appeared shortly afterwards, 'what did you do with the remains of the pigeon from last night?'

'I buried them sir. I felt you would wish me to give the bird a dignified end.'

'Sims, you are an angel. If only all my employees were like you. I need to see the wing feathers. Quick man. Dig the bird up. Get me the feathers. Help him, Peter. Quick now. And get Fowler.'

Half an hour later, DeLuca, Peter and Sims were intently studying the bloody remains of the shot-peppered bird, spread across a piece of newspaper on the desk.

'There,' DeLuca said excitedly, after several minutes of

133

intense concentration, 'a wing bar. No doubt about it. Thank God. Angela didn't take it,' he muttered under his breath.

'Pour me a whisky Sims, there's a good man,' DeLuca asked his butler.

Sims poured out a small whisky and handed it to DeLuca, who sipped it thoughtfully. Peter ran his tongue expectantly around his parched mouth, but waited in vain for DeLuca to offer him a drink. It crossed his mind to help himself, but he thought better of it.

'That'll be all Sims,' DeLuca said, sitting down at his desk. 'Oh, and Sims,' he continued as his butler reached the door. 'Sack Fowler will you? He leaked the story to the press. It was in his eyes. Guilty as hell.'

'The girl from the university must have Rosso,' DeLuca continued when Sims had left the room. 'Fowler said he gave her the birds when Arthur was taken ill. He must have picked up Rosso by mistake.'

'That is awkward,' Peter said helpfully.

DeLuca scowled.

'Let's call it off,' Peter urged, 'We can tell the police and insurance people it was all a mistake. Get the scientist to return the bird and the problem is solved. No one will be any the wiser.'

'And how will I get my money back?'

'I'll think of something. I'll get Antonio to give us a refund. After all we can hardly dress up as animal liberationists and go breaking into the university animal house or wherever they are keeping it, can we?'

DeLuca looked at him and a slow smile spread across his face. 'That's not a bad idea, Peter. Do you think your man is up to it?'

'No. No. No!' Peter said, resolved to refuse any such request. 'I must have been mad to get involved with this business, and I'm not about to become an eco-terrorist, not for anyone. Besides, we don't even know if she has got the bird. Can't you just pay a visit and find out? You bankroll them don't you? Tell them you want to have a look round. It will look perfectly innocent.'

17

Alice had wasted most of Wednesday staring at her computer screen, occupied by her dislike of Joe Landseer. She had replayed to herself on more than one occasion the look on his face as she emptied the bowl of porridge on his head, the memory providing undimmed pleasure. Unfortunately the recollection was invariably preceded by an image which gave her an unexplained empty feeling in the pit of her stomach. This was the view of Joe slipping off Louise's dress in the kitchen. She hadn't taken to Louise. *Only superficial men go for such hard-edge, pretty sorts who wear lots of make-up and dress to show off their legs,* she said to herself. She caught her reflection in the window. *I bet she's a false blond,* she thought defensively as she fingered her own natural chestnut hair, which looked dispiritingly limp compared to Louise's carefully coiffured appearance. She also had to admit that her clothes looked dowdy in comparison to Louise's dress. It must have cost her a fortune, she surmised, for once resenting her meagre research salary. *They deserve each other. I hope I never see him again. He didn't even have the decency to ring and say he was sorry.* 'I positively hate him,' she said fiercely under her breath, glaring angrily at the multi-coloured fish on her screen saver. This conviction was swiftly followed by a feeling of remorse at emptying porridge on Joe's head and a miserable feeling that he would never speak to her again because of it. This in turn was replaced by the memory of being locked in the cellar, and the self-satisfied smirk that Joe had on his face when he'd let her out. It was therefore something of a welcome distraction when her supervisor put his head around the door.

'Mr DeLuca wants to pay us a visit. He especially wants to check that the pigeons are being housed properly, so you better get on to the animal house and make sure the birds are all present and correct. I hope it isn't anything to do with this,' he said, giving Alice a copy of the *Leicester Herald*. 'He's talking about endowing a chair, so we must keep him sweet.'

Alice suppressed a momentary feeling of panic. *Surely he can't have found out about Angela. It must be a coincidence.* 'I don't have to be there, do I?' she asked. 'I was planning a big experiment tomorrow.'

'He especially asked to see you. You've charmed the socks off him. Nine o'clock in my office.'

Alice gave up for the day and walked back to her second-floor flat in an Edwardian brick terraced house about ten minutes from the university across Victoria Park. Her mood of preoccupation deepened as she read the article in the newspaper. However, she was not prepared for Angela's shriek of anguish, accompanied by a torrent of tears as she handed her the paper.

'Angela, don't worry. It will all sort itself out,' Alice said soothingly as the young girl sobbed in her lap.

'You don't understand,' Angela said between spasms of distress. 'No one understands.'

The last thing I need right now is a hysterical teenager on my hands, Alice thought irritably, first blaming Joe and then herself for her foolish impulse to visit him. Looking at Angela's expression of misery, she softened and prepared to be sympathetic.

'I know how you must feel, but I'm sure he does love you. After a few days he'll come round to the idea of you and Mark.'

'He'll never let me and Mark be together, and besides, I've killed his stupid pigeon.'

Alice lifted Angela's head off her lap and looking at her kindly handed her some tissues.

'Now dry your eyes and tell me what a pigeon has got to do with it?'

Angela blew her nose loudly and dabbed her eyes.

'You know Dad and I fell out over Mark, so I had this idea of kidnapping Rosso to make him see sense, but when he found us I threw the bird at him and he shot it. That's why its been reported as lost. It cost Dad fifty thousand quid. He'll never forgive me.' She gave Alice a look of hopelessness and started to cry again. 'Why, oh why was I so stupid? Help me, Alice, you will help me won't you?' she pleaded, looking at her with tear-filled eyes.

'Are you sure it was the prize pigeon that you took?'

'Definitely. I took it from it's cage. All the cages are named. Can't you see? That's why the bird is gone. It's not been kidnapped. I killed it.'

'Your dad killed it. Serves him right for being careless with a gun. I expect it's insured anyway. I tell you what I'll do. I'm seeing your father tomorrow. He's paying a visit to the university. I'll try and sound him out, see what he knows. If he doesn't realise that he shot Rosso it may be OK.'

Angela nodded her head and then started to suck her thumb nervously. 'I've got a confession to make.'

'Oh yes?' Alice said with a feeling of trepidation.

'I rang Mark. He's coming round. He was ever so worried about me. I know you said I shouldn't, but you don't mind, do you?'

'Angela. Do you really think it's wise for him to come here with your picture all over the paper and your father looking for you? You could get me into serious trouble you know.'

'Please.'

'All right, but just a quick visit and he's definitely not staying the night.'

'Oh, and by the way, 'Angela continued as an afterthought, ' I forgot to tell you, Joe phoned yesterday and left a message. Something about being sorry.'

The thought of Joe in a contrite mood stimulated in Alice the idea, that with missing pigeons featuring prominently in the local media, it would be prudent for her to recover the ailing bird from the Waterhouse. *Better a sick pigeon than no pigeon at all,* she thought. She emphatically denied to herself that there was any ulterior motive in paying Joe a visit. Even when she caught herself applying a smidgen of mascara for the first time in months, she failed to confess that her sudden sense of cheerfulness had anything to do with seeing Mr Landseer.

Preoccupied with whether she should be frosty or forgiving towards Joe, it was not until she turned into the field road that led to the Waterhouse that it occurred to her that Louise might still be there. She drove slowly towards the house, stopping just outside the gate to the yard, and got out of the car. Peering around the gatepost through the gathering gloom of the evening, she was heartened to see that there wasn't another car in sight. She walked cautiously towards the house, which was in darkness. *Perhaps they are out,* she thought. A horse whinnied in one of the stables, making her jump. Steeling herself and taking a deep breath, she strode up to the kitchen door and knocked firmly. Immediately she felt overwhelmed by nervousness and ran to shelter behind the trunk of a weeping willow. The light over the door came on and the door opened. Joe looked out. Shrugging his shoulders, he went back in and closed the door. Alice bit her thumb, a trait she had developed in childhood when faced with difficult moments, and walked back to the door. She knocked again and waited. When Joe opened the door she remembered him with porridge dripping down his face and had to suppress a giggle.

'Alice,' he said, a note of warm surprise in his voice.

'I'm sorry,' they said simultaneously.

'I'm sorry about the bowl of porridge,' Alice repeated. 'I was just so mad at being locked in the cellar.'

'*You're* sorry. God, I felt awful. I deserved to be thrown into a bath of the stuff. Come on in out of the cold. No, it's OK,' he continued, seeing a look of anxiety cross her face, 'Louise has gone back to London. I'm on my own.'

Alice felt a sudden sense of elation. Joe showed her into the sitting room where a fire was blazing in the grate. Several teacakes were toasting on a rack, watched with interest from the sofa by Hercule, who was sharing his cushion with a large, well-fed, white-and-orange cat. Alice thought it all looked adorably cosy.

'Would you like a toasted tea-cake? You can have Rutland Organic Honey or home-made strawberry jam to go with it,' he said, holding up two pots for her examination. 'Personally I just like oodles of butter. Louise has made us switch over to some ghastly low-fat spread so I'm treating myself. I'm really pleased you came. I felt terrible about yesterday.'

Alice sat down next to the cat, who stretched out his head in expectation of a rub behind the ears. Alice responded obligingly and gave Hercule a corresponding pat.

'Did everything work out all right with Louise?' she asked awkwardly.

'Fine, actually.' Joe replied, equally uncomfortably.

'Are you still selling the house?'

'Yes. Louise is organising everything. She is very efficient.'

'And how is life as a farmer?' she asked with forced brightness, trying to get away from the subject of Louise.

'Wretched,' he said with a smile. 'Walter had me out all afternoon herding the sheep into the barn. Apparently they are going to lamb any minute. There is no doubt that sheep are completely stupid. There were only ten of them and it took me hours. They do exactly the opposite of what you want them to do. I definitely need a sheepdog if I'm to stay here.'

'But I thought you said you are definitely selling the house?' Alice asked in surprise.

'Yes, so I did,' Joe said uncertainly. 'We've got to. Louise would never leave London.'

Joe leant forward and turned over the teacakes. He then poured out the tea into some pretty china teacups.

'My aunt was very proper. When I stayed with her, no matter what there was to do around the farm, she always insisted on high tea. I have this memory of cold winter nights during the Christmas holidays, snuggling up to the fire, being fed tea from these very cups with loads of sandwiches and cakes and shortbread and all sorts of goodies, while she told me stories of life in Freasby when she was a child.'

'She sounds very sweet.'

'Not sweet exactly. She could be an old dragon, but I think she had a soft heart. What are you doing tonight?' he asked, changing the subject. 'Let me take you out for a meal, to make up for my cruelty in locking you in the cellar. Or better still, let me cook you supper. I'm not a bad cook. Not dangerous anyhow. There are some courgettes and leeks from the garden. I could make a ratatouille of sorts with baked potatoes. Or I could sacrifice a chicken in your honour. I've got some wine. Aunt kept a small but select cellar. Coq au vin, only you'd have to do the slaughtering. I agree, stick to vegetarian,' he said as she held up her hands in mock horror, 'Altogether better for the digestion.'

They dined in the warmth of the sitting room listening to songs by the likes of Sam Cooke, Roy Orbison and Elvis Presley, Joe having found a box of his mother's '45' singles in the loft. They shared accounts of their lives since they left college, discussing the books they would take to a desert island, the films they would want to watch there, provided they had a generator, and the people they would invite to join them. They agreed that the obituaries were the most interesting parts of newspapers, that chocolate was easily the best flavour for ice cream, that surely there must be more to space travel than the discovery of Teflon and that mink farmers should be made to live for a week in one of their cages. They disagreed over whether Jupiter or Saturn was the biggest planet, the relative merits of British and American sitcoms, and whether Alice's eyes were green or grey. By midnight, when they smooched to The Teddy Bears singing *To Know Him is To Love Him*, they both felt they had just spent one of the most enjoyable evenings of their lives.

'God, is that the time? I must go,' Alice said in alarm, looking at her watch. 'I've got this important meeting tomorrow, which reminds me, one of the reasons I came over was to get the pigeon. Mr DeLuca seems to have lost one of his prize birds and I didn't think it would look too good if I didn't have a full complement.'

Joe looked anxious.

'I was hoping you weren't going to ask me that,' he said, blushing. 'I went to feed him after I'd finished with the sheep and he got away. Flew into one of the trees. I was hoping he'd come back of his own accord and I wouldn't have to tell you.'

'Oh,' Alice said, biting her lip uneasily.

'I tell you what,' Joe said eagerly, a solution occurring to him, 'why don't we ask Walter to give you one of his? I'm sure DeLuca can't know what all his pigeons look like.'

'Won't Walter mind being woken up?'

'Probably. But I'm in his bad books anyway from yesterday morning and he likes you. Come on.'

They drove up to the village and knocked up Walter, who scowled at Joe when he opened the door in his pyjamas and a dressing gown, but softened visibly when he saw Alice.

'Now look after him miss,' he said as he handed Alice the pigeon in a wicker carrier.

'Any of those sheep started yet?' he asked gruffly, turning to Joe.

'I forgot to look. I'll see when I go back. What is it? They lie down and turn their heads upwards, is that right?

Walter gave him a despairing look.

'But what happens if it doesn't come out foreleg first, like you said?'

'You help it,' Walter replied, as if it was obvious.

'Great,' Joe muttered to himself.

Alice pulled up by the door of the Waterhouse and switched off the engine. It was a clear night and there was a soft light from a full moon. They sat for a moment in silence, enjoying the rustle of the wind and the sound of the river. A tawny owl hooted in the distance. Joe felt an overwhelming urge to lean across and kiss Alice. They looked at each other. With an effort he resisted his impulse to embrace her.

'I'd better look at the sheep' he said reluctantly, 'although I've no idea what to watch out for, and even less idea what to do if I did. I really think Walter could have been more helpful.'

'It's fairly obvious. You'll know,' Alice replied with a catch in her voice.

'Have you ever seen sheep have lambs?' he asked her.

'Lots. I did a fair bit of lambing at my uncle's place. A few years ago of course.'

'Will you come and look with me?' he asked eagerly.

'OK,' she said with a smile.

Joe guided her towards the barn, gently holding her arm, and then as they approached the door, taking her hand. As he did so, Alice stopped and looked at him, taking his other hand. They were about to kiss when a loud, plaintive bleat came from within the barn.

'That didn't sound too good,' Joe said, with a combination of disappointment and anxiety.

They walked into the small stone barn where ten sheep lay huddled close to each other making soft snuffling noises. Joe switched on the light. One sheep lay separated from the rest. It gave another distressed bleat.

Alice knelt down to examine it. After a few moments she looked up.

'I think it may be a breech.'

Joe looked blank.

'You know, when it comes out back first instead of front first.'

'Is that a problem?'

'You don't know much about babies, do you?'

'Not much,' Joe had to admit. 'Shall I get Walter?'

'I'm not sure we've got time. The sheep looks fairly far gone. The lamb may already have suffocated.' Alice stood up, a decisive look on her face. 'We need hot water, towels, gloves, disinfectant, and some iodine. We'll need a good light too. There must be a lambing pack around somewhere. And put that heater on.'

'I remember Walter said it was all in a cupboard in the kitchen. I'll get it.'

Joe returned a few minutes later with a large pack of materials, a bucket of water and a torch.

'I've put the water on the stove. Here is a bucket of cold water to be going on with.'

Alice rummaged around in the pack and laid the various articles on a towel.

'Good. Now come over here and hold the sheep up with its shoulders resting on the ground. That's right, a bit higher – good.'

Alice quickly put on a pair of surgical gloves and proceeded to insert her hand into the sheep's vagina with a squelching noise, gently feeling for the orientation of the lamb. The sheep twisted in Joe's hands. He started to feel queasy.

'Could you shine the torch?' Alice asked. 'Not there you twit – there, that's right, and don't let it shake so much.'

Joe decided that if it ever came to the point of becoming a father he would forsake current trends and monitor events from the safety of the pub.

'Alice I hate to distract you, but I think I may be about to become re-acquainted with the evening's courgettes.'

'Well you can't be sick yet. I need you to hold on to the sheep. There we go,' she said with a pleased tone as first one, then two legs appeared from inside the ewe. 'Won't be long now.'

Shortly afterwards the rest of the lamb appeared, bottom first. Wet and slimy it looked pathetically limp, but after a rub down with the towel it gave a soft bleat, followed by a more determined cry. Alice looked at Joe with a triumphant smile. Joe smiled back, but then his view of Alice began to fade in a kaleidoscope of stars.

By the time his head had cleared the lamb was suckling contentedly at the mother's teats and Alice was washing her hands in the bucket. She looked at him.

'Congratulations. You are a father.'

Joe wasn't sure that the night's events justified his name on the birth certificate, but nonetheless he felt inordinately pleased. He looked at the little creature, now positively fluffy, concentratedly nuzzling the ewe's tummy, and felt a warm glow of delight.

'Alice, you were absolutely wonderful.' He went over and gave her a heartfelt hug. Then, with an admiring look, he kissed her lightly on the lips. 'You can be my chief shepherd.'

'I'd love that.'

'What do we do now?'

'I should really like to keep an eye on them for an hour or so, just to make sure everything is going OK. The ewe sometimes turns against the lamb after a difficult birth and these first few hours are important.'

'I'll do that,' Joe said. It's 2am. Why don't you stay here?' No, I insist. Much better if you drive back tomorrow morning. Besides, I may need more help. I'll just go and get some blankets.'

When he returned, Alice was asleep on a pile of straw in the corner of the barn. He covered her with a blanket and sat down next to her, savouring a feeling of contentment.

He awoke with Alice in his arms, her head on his shoulder. An early-morning light filtered through the barn door, revealing the indistinct shapes of the sheep huddled together. One of them, chewing on some hay, looked at him unconcernedly. He lay back and listened to the glory of the dawn chorus waxing and waning in concert with the wind rustling in the trees. Alice stirred and opened her eyes. She smiled dreamily.

'What time is it?'

'About six, I should think.'

She sat up and shook straw from her hair.

'I must be going.'

'I'll make us some breakfast. Porridge perhaps?'

She smiled. 'No, I'll wait until I get home. I mustn't be late for this meeting.'

They walked together to her car, unsure how to part. In the end he gave her a kiss on the cheek and she waved goodbye as she drove away.

Had Alice been more awake she might have noticed the man in the dark glasses, sitting in the red Vauxhall Vectra parked outside her flat. However, she couldn't help noticing the handsome young man with dark curly hair who opened the door just as she was putting the key to the lock.

'Hi, I'm Mark,' he said cheerfully. You must be Alice. Looks as if you had a good night,' he said cheekily, and jumping down the stairs two at a time, rapidly disappeared from view.

Alice went in and looked at herself in the hall mirror. She was picking some pieces of straw from her hair when Angela appeared from the bathroom.

'I said he wasn't to stay the night,' Alice remonstrated.

'You can talk,' Angela retorted. 'I'll promise not to tell what's-his-name, Andrew, if you promise not to tell Dad,' With which barbed response, she waltzed into the spare bedroom.

18

'What do you mean, you've kept the animals?' Louise said, with more than a hint of anger in her voice.

Joe winced. He abstractly added a cross to the game of noughts and crosses he was playing in the condensation on the window of the saloon bar of the pub. With a certain distracted satisfaction, he joined three crosses together.

'Well? Have you been struck dumb or something?' Louise continued irritably.

'I don't know. I'd been up all night helping this sheep to have it's lamb and when the lorry came I just didn't have the heart. They were going to take them all to the abattoir, you know.'

'Where on earth did you think they were going? Butlins? They are a lot of old crocks like your aunt. Who would want them for God's sake?'

'But you should have seen this lamb. It was so sweet. And when we found the mother on its side I was so nervous. It must be just like that when you have a baby.'

'We?' Who was with you?' Louise flashed.

'Walter, of course,' Joe said, rapidly collecting himself.

'For goodness' sake, don't go all broody on me. That would be the last straw. You've got to stop being sentimental about this,' she continued more sympathetically. 'I know you like animals, but what happens when we sell the Waterhouse? They'll have to go then. It will only get harder for you the longer you wait. Sooner rather than later is best.'

'Carter said he would look after them.'

'Carter won't do anything that will cost him money. Look, I must go. What time will you get down tomorrow?'

'I think I had better stay up here this weekend. The sheep need constant looking after and I can't ask Walter to do it all.'

'But we've got Richard and Samantha coming round on Saturday and I've got those free tickets to Sadler's Wells,' Louise said disappointedly.

'I'm sorry love, but it's only for this week. After all that was what the doctor ordered, wasn't it? A week or two in the country. Got to go, I'm using the pub's phone.'

'God Joe, why don't you get yourself a proper contract? No wonder you got sacked. How can you hope to be a journalist when you are so hopeless about everything to do with technology?'

'I prefer the personal touch,' replied Joe defensively. 'Anyway, there isn't a signal in the village. I'll ring you tomorrow. Bye. Lots of love.'

Louise tapped her phone against her chin distractedly before touching a contact.

'Mr Carter? It's Louise Smith here, the Waterhouse. I've got the estimates. The highest is eight hundred thousand pounds.'

She wrote 800 on a notepad and doodled around it as she listened into the telephone.

'It may sound a lot, but that was the deal, remember. I'll send you the estimate. I think I should warn you, Mr Landseer is very attached to the Waterhouse. He's always had a sentimental thing about the place. The longer he stays the more likely it is that he won't want to sell.'

She listened again as he complained how much it would cost to do up.

'I know. I'm completely on your side, but Joe never has been very realistic about money. If he wants something he can get very stubborn and ignores the consequences. All I'm saying is that if you want the Waterhouse you had better get going with the lawyers and set the deal up as soon as possible. I'll be in touch.'

Fred Carter put his phone into the pocket of his well worn waxed coat and rubbed his chin thoughtfully with the catalogue of the farm sale he was attending.

'Penny for your thoughts Fred.'

'Hello Ray. Not often we see you at a farm sale these days. I heard you were thinking of selling up.'

'Aye. I reckon so. Can't make ends meet any more. Take the pigs. I got twenty quid a pound last week. That's half what it cost me to feed 'em.'

'It's tough at the moment right enough,' Fred agreed sympathetically, 'Bad as I've known it.'

The two men nodded grimly and looked over their ample paunches at the muddy ground. They were standing in a farmyard which opened out into a paddock where a varied array of farm machinery and implements were laid out in neat lines, each pile of assorted bric-a-brac an item on the auctioneer's catalogue. A smallholder was selling up. He had been in business for fifty years and it looked as if he had kept everything; good, bad and useless. The lots appeared to be arranged at random, with a pile of bald tractor tyres next to a nearly new baler. This was followed by a throaty-sounding 1958 Fordson tractor with twelve thousand hours on the clock. There were about one hundred people in the paddock, gathered together in knots, discussing the weather and intermittently shaking their heads at the state of farming, although the number of new SUVs in the makeshift car park suggested that not everybody was feeling the pinch. In the farmyard, next to the auctioneer's tent, was a mobile cafe which was serving bacon butties and hot tea. The smell of frying bacon wafted over the farmyard, attracting a steady stream of customers. The enticing odours reminded Fred that he had missed his breakfast. There was nothing he liked better than a fried bacon-and-egg sandwich out in the open like this. He glanced up at the sky. A light drizzle had just started.

'Fancy a bite, Ray?'

'I've got my eye on that feeder.' Shouldn't fetch more than a quid or two. Catch you later.'

Fred hunched his shoulders against the rain and walked over to the motorised cafe. He picked up his sandwich and took a large bite, licking his lips to catch every drop of grease and fried egg. He turned to survey the scene, his back leaning against the counter. He had come to buy some cattle, but the livestock were being sold later in the day. He liked these sales. He found it oddly satisfying to see another farmer giving up, throwing in the towel. It made his survival seem more real. It was a chance to catch up on gossip as well. See if any land was likely to come up. Get wind of somebody in trouble so he could go in with a low price. There was always a bargain to be made if you knew where to look. He thought of his conversation with Joe Landseer's girlfriend. He liked her, he decided. Landseer was damp behind the ears, but she was sharp; wouldn't miss a trick. He'd enjoy putting one over on her. He wondered if she was telling the truth about Landseer or whether it was just a bluff.

'Hi Dad. Looks like we're in for even more rain.'

Fred looked at his son, David, who was accompanied by his wife, Jenny. Fred nodded without saying anything. Jenny made him feel uncomfortable. She always looked as if she was accusing him of something. It wasn't his fault they didn't get on. *Miserable bitch,* he thought.

'You're not usually interested in farm sales,' Fred said, turning to Jenny.

'Jenny and I are on our way into Felton,' David explained. 'I wanted to have a look at the Fordson. See if it was worth doing up.'

Jenny gave her husband a disgruntled look and wandered away to the auctioneer's tent.

'I crossed the River Wreake earlier on,' David continued, his mouth half full of a hamburger. 'It were a torrent. Good job they put that overflow into the canal otherwise there'd be flooding. Chevanage's place would get it right and proper, like it used to. I can't think when we last had so much rain.'

Fred looked at his son gratefully as an idea occurred to him. *Out of the mouths of babes and sucklings*, he thought.

'I'm not going up there Walter, and that's that,' Joe said firmly, looking up at the pigeon sitting on a branch of an ash tree that overhung the pond. 'I've had enough of climbing trees for one week. He'll come down eventually.'

'Might fly off,' Walter replied.

'I thought you said he was hurt?'

'Might be hurt, I said. Go on son. It'll be done in a jiffy.'

'No!' Joe said emphatically. 'I don't do trees. What are you doing?' he continued in exasperation, as Walter took off his cap and started to climb the ash.

'Well, if you won't do it I suppose I'll have to risk my old bones. If you give me a lift up I might just be able to reach that first branch.' Walter made a deliberately pathetic attempt to reach a lower branch.

'Oh very well, but if I end up in the pond I'll never speak to you again,' Joe said, and started to climb the tree, feeling a familiar sense of anxiety as he reached a second branch. He climbed gingerly towards the branch where the pigeon was coolly watching his progress.

'Walter, I'm not at all comfortable with this,' Joe said nervously.

'You've done most of it,' Walter said encouragingly, 'he's on the branch just above you. Creep along lad, and if you stand up you can grab him.'

'It's a long way to fall.'

'You're only up a few feet,' Walter said dismissively.

'It may seem like a few feet to you, but from up here it feels like the Eiffel Tower. Anyway, won't it fly away as soon as I get close?'

'I told you, he's hurt his wing. He would have gone by now if he could.'

Joe shuffled his way along the branch he was sitting on. He glanced upward and stared into the beady eye of the pigeon. He was about to secure his position by getting a firm grip of the branch above when his foot slipped on the rain-soaked wood and he lost his balance. Desperately grasping for a hold he ended up swinging, hanging upside down like a giant bat.

'All right lad?' Walter called. 'Can you see the pigeon?'

Joe had a worm's-eye view of the pigeon, which had hopped nimbly onto the branch where he was oscillating. Head cocked to one side he gave Joe a pensive look before hopping from branch to branch and landing by Walter's foot. Walter picked him up and examined him before putting him in a basket.

'I think the wing is bruised but not broken,' Walter reported reassuringly.

'My day is made. Now perhaps you might get me a ladder?'

'Right oh lad. 'Ave you down in a jiffy.'

Walter carried over a ladder and Joe climbed down uneventfully, feeling rather pleased with himself.

'Shall I take it back to Alice?' Joe asked, looking for an excuse to visit her.

'I think I'd better look after him for a bit,' Walter said firmly. 'Check out that wing.'

That Thursday afternoon, Alice opened the door of her apartment, hoping it was Joe. Unfortunately it was DeLuca. She tried to think of some reason why she might legitimately shut the door on him, but although she opened her mouth in preparation for the words to be spoken, no sound emerged.

'Good afternoon my dear. Now, I believe you have something that belongs to me,' With which comment, he pushed past her going into the hall, forestalling any protest. 'Where is she?'

'Who?'

'Don't act the simpleton. My daughter. I had that scumbag nephew of mine followed to your flat.'

Alice decided to try and brazen it out. 'I'm sorry Mr DeLuca,' she said, trying to suppress the quaver in her voice, 'I know you must be upset about your daughter, but you've no right to come barging in here without my permission. I understand that you may feel, because of the grant you gave the university, that you have some authority over me, but I am expecting company and I am afraid I am going to have to ask you to leave.' She looked at him defiantly. He returned her glare with a cool smile.

'You've got spunk, I'll give you that, but I am not leaving without my daughter. Will you tell me where she is, or do I have to search the place?'

'You will do no such thing.' Alice flared up, now genuinely angry. 'I have no idea where your daughter is,' she lied furiously.

'Is that you, Mark?' Angela asked, opening the door of the sitting room. 'Oh my God. It's you.'

19

Joe enjoyed a pleasant evening in the Agricultural, making up the darts team. After weaving his way home and getting soaked by the persistent rain in the process, he fell asleep in an armchair by the stove. On later reflection he wasn't sure whether it was Hercule climbing onto his head, or the water soaking through his shoes that woke him up. Sufficient to say that as dawn was breaking Joe awoke to find the River Wreake in his kitchen.

'This is not good, Hercule,' he said perceptively to his furry companion. Hercule twitched his nose in agreement.

Picking up the rabbit, Joe climbed the stairs to take refuge in his bedroom. Leaning out of the window, all he could see in the grey light was water. The pond had disappeared, merging with the river. The bridge had also gone. It was still raining heavily. He estimated that the barns were flooded to a depth of one or two feet. Above the roaring of the river he could hear an urgent baaing from the sheep and an anxious neigh from the stable. He crossed to the other side of the house, sensing as much as seeing the river rushing past. The water licked the windows of the sitting room, buffeting the house with large pieces of wood and debris that momentarily crashed against the stonework before tumbling on their way.

The house was dividing the river, the main stream following its normal course and a subsidiary channel flowing around the front of the house. What was needed, Joe thought, was a cool head. What was really needed he recognised was some functioning telecommunications. He sat on the bed and tried to think of a plan. The problem was, that alongside his fear of heights, he wasn't very keen on water. Not all forms of water, of course. A soothing hot shower after a hard day at the office was a positive pleasure and he was quite happy to drink the stuff. Indeed, he could even see the point of stretching out for a couple of widths in the heated pool of a five-star hotel. The problem was water in excess, water out of control, water when you couldn't see the bottom. He therefore decided to opt for Plan A. This involved getting into bed, climbing under the bed clothes and nursing his hangover until the rain stopped. He was about to put Plan A into action when he caught Hercule giving him a disapproving look.

'What?' he asked irritably.

Hercule twitched his nose and jumped onto the window sill, cocking his ears. Hercule's vote was clearly for Plan B.

'It's all very well for you,' Joe said grumpily, 'but while I'm out there risking life and limb to rescue a few sheep, who anyway will be on the supermarket shelf in month or two, you're up here enjoying the view. Besides, I would need a boat.'

He then remembered an inflatable boat which he had been given by his aunt one birthday in an attempt to overcome his aquatic phobia. It had been stored in the attic. He climbed into the loft and there it was, just as he remembered, packed in a large box. He dragged it down to the bedroom for further inspection. It had been a large boat for a child, far superior to the average children's toy and he had been enormously proud of it, although it had never got off dry land. From the point of view of an adult it seemed considerably smaller and less sturdy than he remembered. Nonetheless, it looked serviceable, complete with a foot pump and red paddle. He looked out of the window again. Still raining. In the improving light he could see that the field bordering the house was submerged along the length of the riverbank, with water covering the field road for about fifty yards. However, if he could get the animals into the boat and guide them out of the main gate he should be able to get them to safety. *Plan B it is then,* he thought with a malevolent look at Hercule.

He inflated the boat in the kitchen and opened the door. The rush of water almost knocked him off his feet. Dressed in a thin blue anorak and white boxer shorts covered with cerise elephants, he waded outside, pulling his bright yellow boat behind him. He trudged towards the barn which housed the sheep. Opening the door with difficulty, he was confronted by the forlorn sight of ten sheep, paralysed with fear and up to their withers in water, together with the lamb which had managed to climb onto one of the straw bales and was bleating incessantly. He moored the boat against a post and, with all his strength, picked up one of the ewes and lifted her into the boat. She immediately jumped out and started floundering in the water. Joe picked her up again and with enormous effort turned her upside down. Then, tucking the lamb under his arm, he pulled the boat along the submerged path that led out of the yard and through the gate. After about twenty yards the ground started to rise and the water became shallower. With dry land nearby he rolled the sheep out of the boat and watched with satisfaction as she bounded up the field to safety, accompanied by her daughter. *Piece of cake*, he thought smugly.

It now became a race against time as the rising waters threatened to engulf the sheep. As he was rolling the sixth sheep out of the boat it became punctured and rapidly filled with water. He would have to carry them. The water by the barn door now reached well above his knees and the current was strong enough to risk knocking him off his feet. He managed to carry the seventh sheep to safety, but as he passed the gate with the eighth it struggled in his arms. Knocked off balance, he stumbled and fell. The sheep escaped from his grip and ran towards the river. Immediately it was caught up by the current and Joe watched helplessly as it was swept away and lost to sight. He got up, exhausted, and looked about in desperation. With relief he saw a Land Rover coming towards him from the road. Walter and Fred Carter jumped out.

'Christ,' Carter said in amazement, a shocked look on his face.

'The whole place is flooded,' Joe said, trying to catch his breath, 'There are two sheep left in the barn and Harry is in the sty. The horse and donkey are in the stable. I got most of the sheep out, but I think one has drowned. The goat is tethered up by the tennis court. He'll be OK for the moment at least.'

'You look done in,' Carter said sympathetically. I'll get the sheep, can you manage the rest?' he asked Walter, who nodded.

Joe watched as Trigger, the horse, was led to safety and Carter carried one of the sheep out of the barn. Encouraged by this support, Joe went back to look for Harry. Attaching a rope around his neck he started to lead him out of the sty. Although the water almost covered Harry's sturdy little legs Joe had a vague idea that pigs could swim if needs must. He certainly hoped so, because there was no way he was going to pick Harry up and carry him to safety, prize pig or not. Dragging a reluctant Harry, Joe headed for higher ground. However, as he was trying to cross what was now a well defined-stream that ran in front of the barns, a log swept across his legs and made him stagger. Harry pulled the rope out of his hands and started to run back towards his sty, but instead was carried by the current towards the river. Joe stood up and started to wade after him, trying to catch hold of the trailing rope. Suddenly his feet gave way and he plunged into deep water, becoming instantly submerged and swept away by the strong current. Flailing wildly and desperately fighting the urge to open his mouth, he surfaced briefly, taking a gulp of half air, half water before sinking again. He could see nothing. His chest hurt; he needed to breathe. He opened his mouth, but only muddy water entered. He struggled madly, but just couldn't reach the surface. In an oasis of calm he realised that he was going to drown. This felt like a very stupid thing to let happen. He had another go at limb-flailing. This time he felt something brush his arm and grabbed it frantically. A rope. He pulled and felt himself momentarily lifted to the surface. He gulped air before going down again. Keeping a grip on the rope, he used it to guide himself upwards. He reached the surface again and saw that the rope was attached to Harry, who was managing to keep himself afloat with some athletic-looking paddling, although he appeared none too impressed with having Joe along as a partner. Joe, partly supporting himself by gripping the rope close to Harry's head and partly by his own efforts, managed to keep himself afloat and regain his senses. The current seemed to have ebbed slightly, and as they approached a bend in the river both Joe and Harry had the same idea and swam as best they could towards the right-hand bank. Joe managed to grab a large root with his free arm and hauled them both out of the main body of the stream into the shallow waters of the flooded field. Crawling a few yards to safety, he collapsed on his back and stared up at the grey sky. In the distance he could see the Waterhouse and was amazed to see that they had only been carried a few hundred yards. Harry prodded him with his snout and grunted before wandering off.

Joe vaguely heard the sound of a car engine and opened his

20

'Where the hell is my pigeon?' DeLuca asked Peter Garibaldi, banging his desk in frustration.

'How am I supposed to know?' Peter replied defensively.

'Because I pay you to know. My brother is at the bottom of this. That bastard would do anything to get at me. He hates my guts, and after all I've done for him.'

'How's Angela?' Peter asked solicitously.

'Locked in her room. She's let me down Peter. Betrayed me. Going off with that piece of garbage. I don't know what I'm going to do with her. Headstrong, that's her problem. Don't know why. Her mother wasn't like that. I've spoiled her. Well, that's come to an end. Know what I'm going to do?'

Peter shook his head.

'I'm sending her to Italy. Spend a year or two with my sister. That'll sort her out. What do you think?'

Peter shrugged his shoulders non-committally. He felt nervous. He always felt nervous around DeLuca these days. You could never tell where the man was coming from. One minute he was your best friend, the next he would be threatening grievous bodily harm. *I need to get out of his clutches,* he thought. This pigeon thing was getting to him. Trouble was, business hadn't been too good lately. What with one thing and another DeLuca was just about his only big client.

'Well?' DeLuca asked.

'What?' Peter replied blankly, coming out of his reverie.

'Where do you think the bloody pigeon is? Your friend, the criminal mastermind of East Leicestershire, doesn't appear to have it. The bird I smeared over the ceiling wasn't it, that girl from the university doesn't know anything about it, so where the fuck is it?'

'Does it matter?' Peter asked matter-of-factly. 'Why don't we just say the ransom note was a hoax, tell the insurance people the bird was temporarily mislaid and let the whole thing drop? Put it down to experience. You'll hardly miss the money.'

DeLuca beckoned Peter over to the desk.

'Put your hand on the blotter, Peter.'

Peter did as he was told, whereupon DeLuca brought a glass paperweight hard down on the back of his hand.

'Christ!' Peter shouted, holding his hand and grimacing in pain. 'You've broken my hand. What did you do that for?'

'For being a dick head. I'm fifty thousand pounds the worse for wear with that pigeon and I'm not about to "let the whole thing drop", as you put it. Someone is pissing me around with this, and at the moment I regard you as the number one suspect. Now what are you going to do about it?' he finished with an angry shout.

Peter rubbed his hand ruefully and glanced at DeLuca's glowering face. A spasm of nausea washed over him, brought on by the pain in his hand. He felt like walking out of the room and letting DeLuca get on with it.

'You leave this room before I say you can and you're finished,' DeLuca threatened, guessing his intention. 'Now, I reckon that my brother must somehow have got hold of Rosso, so I want you to search his loft.'

'What?' Peter said incredulously. 'I don't know the first

thing about pigeons. I couldn't recognise Rosso from a Barbie doll. Besides, why on earth should your brother have taken it?'

'I don't know,' DeLuca said, coming up close to Peter's face, 'but if you have any better ideas I'd love to hear them. In the meantime, get yourself over to my brother's place and check it out. Remember, Rosso is the pigeon without the wing bars. It should have a ring stamped with RR-1 on it's foot. And don't get caught. Now piss off.'

When Peter had left, DeLuca took up his favourite position by the French windows, looking through the line of cypress trees that marched down the drive. It was early evening and the sun was just setting behind the house, casting long shadows over the neatly clipped lawn that spread towards the road. He felt suddenly very weary. Everything appeared to be unravelling. Both his daughter and his brother hated him. His friends, the few he'd had, were dead or dying, and he had to put up with pip-squeaks like Peter Garibaldi, a disgrace to his father. De Luca felt old and out of touch. His one pleasure, his pigeons, had been all messed up by this Rosso business. Nothing was going right. He felt a deep sense of loneliness and wondered if he shouldn't sell up and retire. Go back home and put his feet up for the few years he had left. He felt a sudden pang for the warmth of his native country, for the smell of olive groves and the sight of the hundreds of swallows and swifts that swooped and swirled around the streets of his village in the summer. Then he shook his head. Who was he kidding? He was just being an old romantic. He was English now. Italy was lost to him. *These winters get you down*, he thought to himself. Turning away from the window, he pulled a lever in the wall.

A few moments later, Sims knocked on the door and walked softly in.

'I'll take my tea now Sims, if you don't mind.'

'Very good sir. Cook has just made some scones. Would you care to partake, sir?'

'Thank you Sims. I would like that very much.'

Later that Friday evening, Arthur was in the Agricultural Inn buying a pint of bitter for his friend Walter.

'Cheers Arthur,' Walter said, holding up his glass in thanks.

'So the young lad nearly drowned you say?' Arthur said, taking a deep draught of his beer.

'It gave me a real turn. It was Harry that saved him. Never seen a pig like him. A proper hero. He's a dead cert if we can get him to the fair in one piece.'

'Waterhouse flood often, does it?'

'Never known it since they fixed the river. A few times before mind, but not since, not for thirty year or more. Here's Stan. He'll bear me out.'

A stout middle-aged man who did odd jobs around the farms came into the pub and nodded at the two men. 'Evening gents. How's that young friend of yours? I heard he was nearly fish food. Not that there are any fish in the Wreake these days,' he continued with a sad shake of his head. 'Too polluted. It's that dye factory at Fileby I blame. It'd be no surprise if those chemicals don't do for the lad. 'E must 'ave swallowed enough to kill an elephant.'

Stan was passionate about fishing and keenly felt that the water quality in the Wreake was the explanation for his poor catch in recent years. In fact the water quality in the river had improved considerably since his youth, although this was more because of the decline in the textile industry than the efforts of the regional water company. His inability to catch fish was more closely related to a sleep disorder caused by his excess weight, which resulted in an unfortunate tendency to fall asleep on the riverbank shortly after casting his line.

'That as may be,' Walter replied. 'They be keeping him in

for a day or two for observation, but he'll be right enough I reckon.'

'Sounds as if he 'ad a lucky escape though,' Stan agreed. 'Now Annie,' he continued good-naturedly to the proprietor of the inn who was listening in on their conversation, 'when are you going to stir yourself and get a thirsty man a drink?'

'You mind your manners, Stan Skinner,' Annie scolded him, 'or you'll be drinking that coloured water they serve up in the Fox.'

'Harry helped 'im of course,' Walter pointed out, returning to the subject at hand.

'So I 'eard,' Stan said.

'He was in the papers you know; photo an' all,' Walter said, pulling out the front page of the newspaper from the breast pocket of his battered red-and-black-check boiled wool coat.

'Who, the lad?' Stan asked.

'No. Harry. For rescuing him. Herald got hold of it. *"Pig rescues man from drowning"*. Front page it were. Here we are.'

Walter flourished the front page of the paper which was dominated by a handsome photograph of Harry. 'He looks a picture doesn't he?' he said proudly.

Stan and Arthur nodded in polite agreement.

''E's a good sort is 'e, this lad of yours?' Stan asked.

'Oh aye,' Walter confirmed. 'A bit too much of the big city in him at the moment, if you know what I mean, but he'll grow out of that with a month or two of Leicestershire air.'

Arthur and Stan both nodded understandingly. They each took a drink of beer and ruminated on the curious idea that anyone would willingly live in London.

'I was saying to Arthur that the Waterhouse don't usually flood since they did that work on the sluice,' Walter said, breaking the silence.

'Mind you, there's been an awful lot of rain,' Arthur interjected.

'Tree came down and blocked it,' Stan said.

'Is that right?'

'Blocked the overflow, just as if someone had put it there. Saw it myself.'

'That's quite a coincidence,' Annie Wright chipped in sardonically from behind the bar.

'Aye, I reckon it is,' Stan agreed, taking another drink of beer and wiping some froth from his lips with the back of his hand.

'Wouldn't surprise me none if a certain person didn't help that coincidence along a bit, naming no names mind,' Annie continued mysteriously.

'What do you mean Annie?' Walter asked, leaning forward on the bar in encouragement.

'What I means is that a flooded Waterhouse is cheaper on the market than one that's dry,' she continued, with a slight pursing of her lips and a nod of her head as if that explained everything.

'Annie, you be talking in riddles again,' Stan said.

'What Annie means is that if you wanted to buy the Waterhouse, a spot of flooding wouldn't hurt to get the price down a bit,' Arthur interpreted.

'Who would do that?' Stan asked.

'You might start by asking whose land surrounds that house,' Annie replied.

'Fred Carter,' Stan said incredulously, 'Are you saying Fred Carter would deliberately flood the Water'ouse?'

'As I said, I don't name no names. Now gentleman, can I refresh your glasses?' with which she disappeared down the steps into the cellar.

'You know, there might be something in what Annie says,' Walter said thoughtfully. 'Carter would stop at nothing to get my Harry out the way so he can win the fair with his pig.'

'I can't believe it,' Stan said, shaking his head. 'Carter's as tough as shoe leather, but he wouldn't pull a trick like that over a few acres of land, or a pig either.' he continued, giving Walter a pitying look. 'That Annie. She don't 'alf stir.' With which decided comment, he wandered off for a game of darts.

Walter and Arthur picked up their refilled glasses and went over towards the fire, settling down in two easy chairs. They stared at the glowing embers of the logs, supping their beer, content to sit in silence for a few moments.

'You've been in the wars yourself I hear,' Walter said finally.

'Aye. Thought I was on the final journey for a moment or two, but it turned out to be just something they call... hang on a minute I've got the paper here; *acute coronary syndrome,*' he continued proudly. 'I'm on tablets mind and I've got to take things easy. They going to do some tests. A warning they called it. It got the wind up me right enough though. Still, there's a silver lining. That jumped-up little twerp Derek messed up while I was in hospital and got himself the sack.'

'I heard there had been some trouble up at DeLuca's place,' Walter said airily, trying not to sound too interested.

'Rosso's disappeared. Kidnapped they say. Been a ransom note and all, but it all seems a bit fishy to me. Never heard of a kidnapped pigeon before, and coming after me telling the gaffer that the bird is a non-starter in the breeding stakes, I wouldn't wonder if he hadn't arranged it all himself. He isn't afraid of cutting a few corners and he hates to lose money. Thing is,' he continued, leaning forward and lowering his voice, 'I reckon I was wrong about Rosso's tendencies. I think he's batting for the home team. That bird he was fond of, the one I thought was a cock, well, it's just laid a clutch of eggs. My eyesight, that's the problem. Truth is, I'm as blind as a bat with these cataracts. I'll have to resign of course, when DeLuca finds out.' Arthur sat back and morosely took a drink of his beer. 'Whatever though, Rosso's gone and no mistake. 'Ere, what do you make of this?' He handed over a piece of

21

Joe was enjoying being an invalid, although the first few hours had been rather trying. He had been dumped on a trolley for half the morning in the corridor of the A&E department of the hospital, which looked out over the prison and shared many of its features. He had then been shunted into the corner of an old Nightingale ward, which was suffused with the mixed odour of bedpans and disinfectant so peculiar to hospitals. His mood hadn't been improved by an incessant background chatter of coughs, groans and wheezes, the harbingers of disease and death. He was on the point of self-discharging when he was suddenly whisked into an ambulance and transferred to an altogether nicer, modern hospital, on the outskirts of the city. He was placed in a side room complete with en-suite facilities and a window which faced onto a courtyard, resplendent with a profusion of blue and green pansies. It was here that he was discovered by the reporters from the *Herald*. His relative youth and semi-celebrity status made him a pampered favourite with the largely female nursing staff, who undertook his observations with particular diligence. He had slept well, and the nurse who came in to take his mid-morning observations found him in cheerful spirits; breakfasted, washed and sitting up in bed. Joe quickly adjusted the nasal tubing which piped oxygen into his lungs.

'I saw you putting your oxygen on as I came into the room. You should have it on all the time you know,' the charge nurse, a middle-aged man with a gruff, efficient manner, admonished him sternly.

Joe, who had been expecting the comely young female nurse who had plumped his pillow and taken his blood pressure first thing that morning, felt a little put out. 'Has Kylie abandoned me?'

'She was on night duty. Why, aren't I pretty enough for you?' the nurse replied without a smile as he brusquely picked up Joe's wrist to take his pulse, an altogether less pleasant experience than the gentle caress of his previous attendant.

'When can I go home?'

'When the doctors say so.'

'And when will that be?'

'I don't know. Not till after the weekend at least. You've got a patch on your X-ray. Your oxygen level is low and you've still got a temperature. Now, can I get you anything?' he finished in a more kindlier tone, noticing Joe's disappointment.

'Can I make a phone call?'

He drew the portable telephone towards him and dialled. 'Hi Louise.'

'Joe?' a sleepy voice said.

'Sorry. Have I woken you up? I'm in hospital. I almost drowned. I tried to ring you last night.'

'Joe, what have you been doing? You don't sound ill. Which hospital?'

'Valley Meadow, I think it's called. I'm on the respiratory ward. The Waterhouse was flooded and I was trying to save Harry and got swept away in the river. I'm lucky to be alive. I was in the paper.'

'Who, is Harry?'

'You know, the Gloucestershire Old Spot that's going to win the Spring Fair.'

'You sound hysterical. Are you really ill? In danger I mean.'

'No. I don't think so. I feel all right. I reckon it's just a precaution, although these doctors never tell you anything.'

'Good, then I don't need to come up?'

'No I suppose not,' Joe said, feeling that he wasn't garnering quite the level of sympathy that he had expected.

'Oh Joe, don't go all sorry for yourself on me. I'm fed up with driving up to Leicestershire mopping up behind you, literally this time. Besides, I can't put Richard and Sam off now, especially as I've invited Jamie Levitt round to make a foursome. If you had come down for the weekend this would never have happened.'

'And who, is Jamie?' Joe asked suspiciously.

'You know, that new guy at work I told you about. Anyway I must dash. Let me know when they are discharging you. Bye, lots of love.'

Jamie? Jamie?! Not that man she described as the 'dish of the day'? he thought with alarm. *The one with the George Clooney looks, the Einstein-sized brain and the Oscar Wilde wit? The one with the charm of Casanova and the morals to match.* He had to get going. Nip this in the bud. He climbed out of bed and started to put on his socks, but felt suddenly dizzy and was forced to lie down, his cheerfulness rapidly evaporating.

He was distracted by a hesitant knock on the door and looked up to see Alice coming in. She was dressed in jeans and an oversized dark woollen coat that made her look unusually vulnerable.

'Alice,' he said with a bright smile.

'Hello Joe,' she said warmly, giving him a peck on his cheek, removing her coat and depositing a box of Liquorice Allsorts on the locker. 'I read about you in the paper. It sounded awful. Isn't it amazing the way the pig jumped in and rescued you?'

Joe had been distinctly miffed at the way his role in the River Wreake affair had been completely distorted by the *Herald*. Instead of his own heroism being celebrated, he was having to play second fiddle to a pig. He was on the point of correcting this false impression when he was struck by Alice's downcast appearance. Instead of the usual sparkle in the eye and rosy glow on the cheeks she was looking decidedly pale and drawn.

'Come and sit here,' he said, patting the bed next to him, 'where I can see you. I tried to call you on Thursday night.'

'I was out.' Andrew has come back a week early.

'Is everything OK?' he asked solicitously.

'No. Not really,' she said dejectedly, biting her lip. 'Mr DeLuca found out that Angela was staying with me. He thought I had encouraged her to run away. He was foul. God, he's a horrible man, and I thought he was nice. He shouted and ranted. Dragged poor Angela off as if she was his slave. I don't blame her for trying to get away. He said he wouldn't pay my salary any more so I've resigned. I've decided to go off with Andrew to America. Have children and be a good wife. I can see I never was cut out for science.'

'Alice, that's terrible. You poor thing. What a bastard. It wasn't your fault. I'll go and talk to him.'

'It's no use. Stephen, my boss, tried his best, but he wouldn't budge. He's just a horrible old man,' she said fiercely. 'A bully.'

'But they can't make you go, can they? What about your contract?'

'DeLuca was about to give a big grant to endow a professorship for Stephen. He said he wouldn't do that unless I went. I couldn't let Stephen down. Anyway, it's made up my mind about whether I should go with Andrew, so at least that is something.'

'Oh, Alice,' Joe said with feeling, taking both her hands in his and looking at her tenderly. At this point she burst into tears.

He drew her towards him and hugged her to his chest while she sobbed piteously. After a few minutes she stopped crying and looked up at Joe shamefacedly.

'I'm sorry. I'm not usually a cry baby. And look, I've made your pyjamas all wet,' she said, picking at an admittedly rather damp area near his left lapel. 'It's just that Andrew hasn't been at all sympathetic. He's just pleased that I'll be going to America. I haven't been able to let myself go, and I really did want to get my PhD.' At which point, her voice trembling, she started crying again, this time getting his right lapel wet. This was however, a minor discomfort set against the warm glow Joe felt at being able to comfort his friend. As she rested against him, her tears having ceased, he ventured a kiss on the crown of her head. She drew back and gave him shy smile. Joe gave her a tissue and she wiped her eyes and blew her nose.

'You're really sweet, Joe. It's not many men who would let almost complete strangers cry all over them. Most men seem to run a mile from emotion. Andrew can be so stiff sometimes,' she finished with feeling, going over to the sink and splashing cold water on her face. She examined herself in the mirror.

'Look at me. Anyone can see I've been crying and now I feel embarrassed,'

'Don't be silly,' Joe said reassuringly. 'I'm the one who should feel awful. If anyone is to blame, it's me.'

'That's not true,' she replied, coming back to the bed and this time taking his hands in hers. 'Not really. It's just bad luck.'

'What will you do now?'

'Go home to Devon I suppose, and wait for the visa to come through, although Andrew wants to get married before he goes in May to make it easier. Anyway, I can't afford to stay in my flat and Andrew's place is full of scientists who do nothing but talk about work. I couldn't stand that at the moment.'

'Come and live at the Waterhouse. You could help me get it

straight after the flood and teach me how to be a smallholder.'

'I don't think Andrew would approve of that,' she said with an attempt at a smile. 'I think he's a bit jealous of you already. In fact, I must go. I said I would meet him for coffee at eleven and he doesn't like me to be late.'

They held hands and looked at each for a moment. Then Alice let go and stood up.

'I really must go,' she said reluctantly.

'When will I see you again?'

'I'm not sure. I'll try and let you know what happens. Do you have an email address?'

'I had one at work' Joe said. 'I'm sharing Louise's at the moment.

'I'll send you a wedding invitation,' she said, attempting to be light-hearted, but this only resulted in her eyes beginning to glisten again. 'Good luck with the Waterhouse, and I hope it works out with Louise,' she finished, her voice breaking.

He held out his arms and they embraced, finally allowing each other a lingering kiss which mixed desire with sorrow. They were disturbed by a knock on the door. Alice quickly stood up, smoothed back her hair and picked up her coat. Walter came in holding a bunch of daffodils. Alice blushed.

'Hello Miss,' he said in his deep-toned Leicestershire brogue. 'You two are busy. I'll come back later.'

'No Walter, I'm just off. How is the pigeon?'

'Well, he's not too bad. Nothing serious, although he is pining about something. Like he was lovelorn. Would you like him back?'

'If you don't mind could you keep him for the moment? Things have become a bit complicated. Joe will explain. It's been a great pleasure meeting you,' she said, shaking his hand in a manner that suggested she did not expect to meet him again. 'Goodbye both of you.'

'She's a nice young thing,' Walter said warmly when she

had gone. 'I noticed that you two seemed to be getting on,' he added with a mischievous grin. 'Now, how are you young sir? You look better than you did yesterday morn.'

'I'm all right, but it's terrible about Alice. She's been sacked and it's all my fault. You know that girl Angela? DeLuca found her at Alice's flat and cut off her money. She's had to leave her job. What's worse, she's going to marry some boffin and go off to America. I'm sure she doesn't love him. We must do something.'

'Is that right? That is a bad do,' Walter agreed, running his hand across the back of his neck with genuine concern. 'I've heard tell that this DeLuca 'as a temper on 'im. Tell you what. I'll ask around. See if I can't do something.'

'Thanks Walter,' Joe said politely, although without much belief in his friend's influence. He sank back against his pillow, feeling depressed. 'The Waterhouse is a mess I suppose?'

'Still underwater most of it. Aye, a mess all right. Still, it's happened before; it'll clean up right as rain, if you pardon the pun. Harry's in good shape you'll be pleased to know. Proper hero he is. Did you see him in the paper? That'll do his chances at the show no harm.'

Joe, who suspected that Walter had helped to spin the story in Harry's direction, reacted coolly to this news.

'Are the animals safe?'

'Aye. Carter's looking after most of 'em. Annie from the pub has the rabbit and the cat, and I'm taking care of Harry of course.'

'It's good of Carter to take them in.'

'Aye,' Walter said, sounding none too convinced.

'Do you know why the place flooded?'

'Tree came down. Blocked the overflow. Anyhow,' Walter continued, visibly ill at ease in a hospital environment, 'I'd best be getting along. Just making sure you're in one piece. I brought you some daffs from the garden and the wife made you a cake.'

He produced a large red tin from a canvas holdall. 'She told me to say as you would be welcome to stay until the Waterhouse gets right.'

'That's very kind Walter, but I think I might have to go back to London. Louise is missing me you know. I probably won't come back until the sale is sorted out.'

'You've still a mind to sell then?' Walter said, obviously disappointed. 'I thought you was taking to the place.'

'I was Walter,' Joe replied, feeling guilty, 'but what with the flood and this business with Alice… It's such a good offer. I don't know,' he finished lamely.

A few moments of awkward silence went by until Walter got up from the chair and moved towards the door.

'I'll be off then.'

'Thanks for coming Walter. Give my regards to Mrs Bramley.'

Walter closed the door, stroking his chin thoughtfully. It was time to give the lad a hand.

That afternoon Walter walked into the Ladbrokes betting shop in Felton. Four punters were in the shop. One was playing the fixed-odds machine, two were studying the form in the pages of the Racing Post and the fourth was watching a race on the television monitors, encouraging his investment with a varied mix of exhortations. Walter walked up the counter and handed a betting slip to the middle-aged woman with dyed black hair and extravagant lipstick who was taking the bets.

'It was last week. Fifty-five pounds to come back I believe,' he said politely.

Without a word she picked up the slip and went over to the corner of the counter where she started to leaf through a sheaf of similar slips. After going through them twice she opened a ledger and studied it for a moment before going into an office at the back of the shop. She came out with a small man of about fifty. He was bald and wearing glasses. He also looked at the ledger and then came over to Walter looking at him with a cautious smile.

'I'm sorry sir. I think there has been some sort of mistake. This bet has already been collected.'

Walter gave him a puzzled look.

'How can that be, since I've got the slip here?'

A gentleman came in and said he had lost the slip. His handwriting matched our copy, so we paid him. That's our policy.'

'Who was this gentleman?'

'The manager of the shop glanced down at the ledger. 'A Mr Martin. Ten Oak Tree Road.'

'I thought as much,' Walter said with a weary shake of his head. 'My cousin up to his old tricks again. He can copy my handwriting a treat you know. Well, I won't trouble you no more. It's a family matter.' And, picking up the betting slip which lay on the counter and tipping his hat, he left the shop.

Oak Tree Road was a terrace of farmworkers' cottages that had once been on the edge of Felton. It was now encircled by a large estate of detached red-brick houses, which had been built in the surrounding fields at the time of a royal wedding and christened with such addresses as Windsor Drive and Balmoral Close. Neat, well maintained and spotlessly clean, the estate contrasted sharply with the ex-council-owned cottages, some of which suffered from a general air of neglect. Number 10 was even more unprepossessing than it's neighbours. A 1960s post-office van was parked outside, and a rusting caravan with a semi-detached roof that flapped in the wind stood in what should have been the front garden. Walter opened the gate and walked up the gravel path, knocking firmly on the red plywood front door. After a few minutes it half-opened and then opened wider as the occupant was reassured that his visitor wasn't obviously hostile.

'Codger Martin, isn't it?' Walter said, tipping his hat. 'I believe I was at school with your dad. May I have a few words?'

22

It was Sunday before Peter Garibaldi ventured out in search of Cosimo DeLuca's pigeon loft. He knew that he lived in Knessington, a village about ten miles from Felton. After watching Leicester City lose one-nil to Newcastle he drove out to the village, arriving just as the sun was setting. He realised when he got there that he didn't have the address. He had somehow imagined from the size of DeLuca's lofts that a house with a pigeon loft would stand out, but driving around the village he couldn't see anything obvious. Not even an ice-cream van. He tried to ring DeLuca, but Sims told him he was out.

Knessington was a small, prosperous village in the middle of High Leicestershire, the only area in this part of England that boasted elevations above two hundred feet. It contained a mixture of handsome stone houses, comfortable-looking brick cottages, a few modern bungalows, a terrace of council houses, and one or two mansions occupied by scions of the local hunt. There was a pub, the Huntsman; a shop which doubled as a sub-post office, and a Montessori school. Fewer than half the residents were linked to farming. Despite this economic semi-detachment from rural life, the village was a close-knit and stable community, with a strong identity. This was built around the church, the Women's Institute and a sense of being in the

179

heartland of England, both geographically and psychologically. Knessington had a central square from which radiated roads to Felton, Leicester and a couple of other villages. The houses of the village were strung along these lanes, becoming ever more dispersed as the periphery of the village was reached.

After driving around fruitlessly for half an hour, Peter returned to the square and parked his Jaguar in front of the pub. He felt in need of a drink. His feet were still cold from watching the game and he far from relished this wild goose chase in the depths of the country. He found no pleasure in the aesthetic qualities of English villages. He thought the countryside bleak at this time of year, and country people, like country pubs, stuffy, boring and sanctimonious. He could never understand why the DeLuca brothers wanted to live in the country, with its intrinsic distrust of foreigners. Putting on his sheepskin jacket, he reluctantly left the warmth of his car and walked into the pub, which had just opened. There was nobody either in the lounge or behind the bar. Peter took a seat and waited, impatiently drumming his fingers on the counter. The fire wasn't lit and the lights hadn't yet been switched on, so the place had a cold and gloomy air. He scanned the room. There were a few old photographs of the village on the walls, a single horse brass hung on one of the wooden pillars and some hunting prints, but he could see neither a juke box nor a slot machine. The place confirmed his prejudices about the dullness of rural hostelries. He felt overwhelmed by a feeling of intense irritation.

'Is anybody going to sell me a drink?' he called out loudly.

An overweight man in his fifties appeared from a door behind the bar breathing heavily.

'Hold your horses son,' he replied curtly. 'Just getting the beer on. Now what can I get you?'

'Whisky and soda. No ice.'

Peter finished his drink in two swigs. He sat for a few

moments enjoying the burning feeling in his gullet, followed by a sensation of warmth that spread across his body.

'I'll have another of those,' he requested, less abruptly.

He toyed with his drink, watching the bartender as he washed some glasses.

'You don't happen to know where a man called Cosimo DeLuca lives, do you?' he asked.

The man looked at him without answering.

'He sells ice cream,' Peter added helpfully. 'Lives in this village somewhere.'

'And who might you be?'

'A friend of his. There's a tenner in it for you,' Peter replied, placing a note on the bar.

'I would have thought a friend of his would know his address,' the bartender replied, pushing the note back before disappearing through the door.

'Dumb country bastards,' Peter said under his breath. He would have to get the address from DeLuca after all. Finishing off his drink he got up to go. As he was leaving the pub he bumped into a young man coming through the door.

'Watch where you're going,' Peter said brusquely.

'Sorry, I didn't see you,' the lad replied looking at him apologetically. 'Oh, it's you.' he said, changing his tone to one distinctly more hostile. 'What are you doing here?'

Peter recognised Cosimo DeLuca's son, Mark. A chance encounter in Leicester during the brief period of his affair with Angela had resulted in a rather frosty introduction. Not wishing to exchange pleasantries, he hurried past without replying and drove off, parking his car around the corner in sight of the pub. After about half an hour he saw Mark leave the pub and walk down the hill in the direction of Felton. Peter got out of the car and followed at a distance, keeping to the shadows, making sure he wasn't seen. He saw the youth enter a small house on the edge of the village. Across the road from the house, at the corner of a paddock, he noticed a small wooden hut with a wire cage at the front. Walking up to it, he saw a number of pigeons inside. He had found Cosimo's loft, an altogether humbler structure than his brother's he thought. There were no street lights and the sky was overcast so it was now almost completely dark. Looking around, he put on a pair of gloves and a balaclava which he pulled from his coat. He shined a pencil torch on the door. It was fastened by a small padlock and chain fixed into the door frame with a U-shaped nail.

The frame was half rotten and it was the work of a moment to take a screwdriver, brought for the purpose, and wrench the padlock away from the frame. He entered the hut and methodically searched the loft for a pigeon without wing bars. There were only about twenty birds in the loft, and after fifteen minutes Peter was convinced Rosso wasn't amongst them. He extricated himself from the loft and tried to shut the door, which was ill fitting and wouldn't close properly without the padlock. Sucking his teeth in irritation and looking nervously over his shoulder at Cosimo's house, he leant a large stick against the door to hold it in place and walked quickly back to his car, feeling pleased with himself.

Had he stayed a little longer, he would have seen a gust of wind knock over the stick, leaving the door to swing ajar. However, he would have had to have kept an early-morning vigil to have seen the fox, who had long noted that the pigeons would make a tasty dinner, pad softly up the paddock, prise open the door and enter the avian larder.

23

DeLuca was dreaming. In his first dream he was driving an ice-cream van and the jingle was going round and round in his head. He woke up in a cold sweat. As he surfaced from his sleep, he could still hear the sound of the van echoing around his bedroom. He got up and looked out of the window, almost convinced that there really was a van outside. It was still dark, although dawn was just breaking, a red glow appearing in the eastern sky. Shaking his head, he went to the toilet and then went back to bed, drawing the bedclothes tight about him. He dozed fitfully. Now he dreamt he was having a picnic with his wife on a sultry summer day, lying in a field by a river, soaking up the sun. Suddenly a swarm of bees came down, buzzing around his head. He tried to clear them but they wouldn't go, buzzing louder and louder. He woke with a start, waving his arms to protect himself from the imaginary insects. Realising it was a dream, he lay back, panting, but the buzzing noise continued.

Then it stopped, and there was a loud crash. DeLuca got out of bed and went to the window. Dawn had broken, but the morning was misty and all he could see were the vague, but familiar outlines of the garden and the trees lining the drive. Then, as peered through the mist, he saw that something was wrong, very wrong. Two of the trees were missing. Then the buzzing started again, and he saw the shape of a man, crouching at the foot of one of the trees. The tree suddenly started to bend at a crazy angle and the man danced away. A cold feeling gripped DeLuca's chest. The man was his brother and he was holding a chainsaw. He watched in horror as the tree toppled to the ground.

'Timber,' his brother shouted gleefully and taking a long swig from a bottle, he brandished his chainsaw in the air and ran across the drive to another tree.

DeLuca scrabbled to open the window. 'Stop it,' he shouted, anguish mixing with fury. 'Stop or I'll kill you.'

Cosimo looked up and, giving his brother a two-fingered salute, settled down to work on the next tree. DeLuca flung himself under his bed and pulled out his shotgun. Checking it was loaded, he pointed it out of the window and fired both barrels. Splinters of wood came off the tree just above Cosimo's head. Cosimo, unperturbed continued sawing until the tree started to topple, and then tripped away down the drive, disappearing into the mist. The buzzing noise started again. DeLuca took a handful of bullets from a drawer in his chiffonier and, putting on a dressing gown and slippers, hurried down the stairs, reloading as he did so. He ran out of the house and down the drive towards the noise of the chain saw, firing blindly in the mist. He screamed in agonised distress as he saw the jagged teeth of his beloved avenue.

Suddenly, out of the fog, he saw his brother. He was leaning against a fatally wounded tree, catching his breath, the chainsaw dangling at his side. They faced each other, panting. DeLuca's dressing gown hung open and his slippers were soaked with the morning dew.

'Are you mad?' DeLuca said, 'I'm going to kill you for this.'

Cosimo walked over to a hessian bag lying on the ground. Picking it up, he shook out the contents. The blood soaked carcasses of a dozen pigeons lay scattered on the grass. 'You couldn't stand it, could you?' he said bitterly, his voice thick with drink, 'You couldn't let me enjoy the one thing I can call my own. Look at this bird.' He picked up one of the pigeons. One wing was missing and there was a large, jagged wound in its neck. 'I bred this bird. It was a winner. It could have matched any one of your birds, bought with your dirty money. You killed the thing I loved, so now I'm killing the thing you love.'

'You're mad,' DeLuca said contemptuously. 'Don't blame me if you can't keep the foxes out. You were probably so drunk you forgot to lock the door.'

'You broke into my loft.'

'Rubbish,' DeLuca said uneasily, ' I was here all night.'

'Oh *you* wouldn't do it. You never get your hands dirty. Always someone else takes the rap. I know how you work. Remember, I was one of your henchmen. No, it wasn't you. It was that stinking ponce of a lawyer you've got licking your backside. My boy saw him, snooping around Knessington, asking for my address. What do you say to that?'

DeLuca shrugged his shoulders.

'I don't know anything about it.'

Cosimo looked at him in disgust and, picking up his chainsaw, started on the tree again. DeLuca fired a warning shot at the ground. Cosimo gave a loud roar and suddenly rushed at his brother, threatening him with the saw. DeLuca turned and ran, slipping and sliding on the wet grass, trying to reload as he dodged the wild gyrations of the saw. They weaved in and out of the trees, tripping on fallen branches, acting out a grotesque game of tag. Cosimo, his breathing coming in desperate gasps, aimed a final lunge at DeLuca, slipping as he did so, the chainsaw spinning away into the grass.

DeLuca stood over him. The two brothers looked at each other, consumed with hatred. DeLuca felt a cold, unbearable anger sweep over him. Holding the gun by the barrel he brought it crashing down on his brother's curled-up body. He steadied himself for a second blow, but before he could bring the gun down, from out of the mist, Mark appeared running at full tilt. He tackled his uncle to the ground. The gun fired into the turf and fell from DeLuca's grasp. As he tried to scramble towards it, Mark lifted him up and punched him hard in the face and again in the stomach. DeLuca slumped down, defeated.

Mark picked up the gun and threw it as far away as he could. Then he picked up the chainsaw and stopped its awful scream. As he caught his breath, Angela came running down the path, followed by Sims. She threw herself into Mark's arms, kissing him eagerly. Cosimo got up on his knees and, picking up the chainsaw, started to crawl towards DeLuca, trying to start the saw as he went. Mark gently detached himself from Angela and went over to his father, lifting him up and taking the saw away.

'Get into your van, Dad,' he said wearily, 'Get in and try and get warm. I'll be along in a minute, and don't go anywhere,' he ordered, 'You've done enough damage for one day.'

He then crossed over to DeLuca, who was sitting on the grass staring at the ruin of his avenue.

'I'm taking Angela,' Mark said firmly and coldly. 'Don't try and follow us. My father has got a whole dossier on you, and I won't have any qualms about using it. You might not go to prison, but they certainly wouldn't renew your membership of the Rotary club.'

Then, putting his arm around Angela, he walked off into the mist. Sims went over to DeLuca, and putting a coat around his shoulders, helped him to his feet.

'Come on in sir, and get warm. I'll get Cook to make you a nice cup of tea.'

24

DeLuca was sitting, brooding by the fire, when Sims ushered Walter into his study later that morning.

'I thought I said I wasn't to be disturbed,' he said morosely, looking up at the unprepossessing figure of his guest.

'This is the gentleman who telephoned about the pigeon, sir,' Sims replied politely.

'Oh. Right. Thank you Sims. Well,' he continued, turning his attention to Walter, 'out with it.'

'Walter placed a wicker basket on the coffee table, but remained standing. 'I believe this belongs to you,' he said.

He opened the basket and produced Rosso, whom he handed carefully to DeLuca. DeLuca gently took the bird and examined it expertly, inspecting his plumage, staring intently at the eyes and beak before finally examining the ring on one of his feet. Finally he smiled.

'I am indebted to you sir,' he said, 'The bird has been well looked after.'

'I keep a few pigeons myself,' Walter replied, his demeanour warming slightly in response to this flattery. 'He bruised his wing, but otherwise I think he is well enough.'

'If you would like to see Sims, he will see you are recompensed for your trouble,' DeLuca said, pressing a bell by the side of the fireplace.

'That's not quite all,' Walter said firmly. 'I wonder if you could call in your loft man, Arthur. I believe he has something to tell you.'

DeLuca looked at Walter suspiciously.

'I am a very busy man.'

'It won't take a moment.'

When Sims came in he was asked to summon Arthur. The two men looked at each other in silence until he arrived. Arthur glanced at Walter with surprise when he entered, but then gave him a friendly nod. DeLuca stood up with his back to the fireplace.

'You two know each other I see,' DeLuca observed. 'Your friend has found Rosso,' he informed Arthur.

'Arthur,' tell him about the mistake,' Walter said.

Arthur gave Walter a look of alarm.'

'Go on Arthur. It will turn out all right,' Walter insisted.

'I got it wrong about Rosso being queer an all. The bird he was fond of was a hen. It's just laid a clutch. It's my eyesight. It's none too good and—'

'What?!' DeLuca roared. ' You got it wrong? I should have bloody well known,' he muttered to himself before turning back to Arthur, his face getting redder by the second. 'You bloody fool. You arrogant, opinionated Yorkshire git. Do you know how much trouble you've caused me? Well you can pack your bags right now. I never want to see you around here again. You stupid old bastard.'

Arthur, his eyes downcast started to edge out of the room.

'Stay here Arthur. We haven't quite finished yet,' Walter said firmly. 'Now Mr DeLuca,' he continued in a conversational tone. 'What do you think the insurance company would think if they knew that you arranged to kidnap Rosso? I've had a nice long chat with a Mr Martin, an acquaintance of yours I believe, or at least of your lawyer's. He put me in the picture. Even gave me a signed statement.' He waived a piece of paper at DeLuca.

DeLuca looked cautiously at Walter. 'How much do you want?' he asked wearily.

'I'll take the weight off my feet, if you don't mind,' Walter said, settling into an arm chair. 'Sit down Arthur. First of all, I want you to re-instate the girl, Alice, at the university. She did you a good turn, taking in your daughter. You had no right to get her sacked. And while you are at it give her a pay rise. Second, Arthur here keeps his job, and I suggest you use some of your money to get his cataracts fixed as soon as possible.'

'And what about you? I don't suppose you want to leave empty-handed.'

'I'll take the outcome of one of those eggs that Arthur was mentioning. I haven't had a good bird in a year or two. I fancy a turn with a champion's brood.'

'And if I chuck you out on your ear?'

'I go to the police and the insurance company. I understand the tax man may be interested as well.'

'It's my word against some country bumpkin's.'

'You might get away with it,' Walter agreed, 'but from what I hear, you don't want people prying too closely into your affairs. At the least, your pigeon days would be over. I would see to that. My way, you get Rosso back at full value, no questions asked, and you don't spend much more than if this had never happened.'

'How do I know you won't be back for more next year?'

'I'm no blackmailer Mr DeLuca. Just trying to help out a few friends. Shake on it and you won't hear from me again, I can assure you of that. Arthur will keep his mouth closed, I'm sure.'

Arthur nodded his head vigorously in assent.

DeLuca relaxed and smiled. 'Well, it looks as if you've carried the day, Mr...?'

'Walter.'

They exchanged a firm handshake.

'I'm a man of my word. I'll see the girl right. To tell you the truth, I liked her. As for you,' DeLuca said, turning to Arthur, 'it's lucky you've got some good friends is all I can say.'

25

When Joe was discharged on the Monday morning he couldn't face the thought of seeing the Waterhouse. He rang Mrs Morgan and asked her to organise the insurance and cleaning. Then he caught the train to London. For two weeks he moped about the house, pretending to be convalescent, waiting for Carter and Louise to organise the sale. London irritated him. It was too busy and too crowded. Millions of anonymous faces hurrying about their daily tasks, like worker ants, sardined into the Tube; pushing, shoving, eating, drinking and sweating. Each with their own personal list of loves and hates, obsessions and secrets. After Leicestershire the air tasted of pollution and the down-at-heel ambience of the South London borough where he lived depressed him whenever he ventured out. He was oppressed by a sense of displacement, an ill-defined feeling of unease that he put down to post-traumatic stress disorder. He was poor company, and Louise soon lost her sympathy with his disconsolate mood. It was a relief when Mrs Morgan rang to say the contracts were ready to be exchanged. It could have been done by post, but Joe felt he wanted to see the Waterhouse one last time. He was to go up the night before, and Louise agreed to come up and meet him in Felton the next morning.

He had decided to sleep in the Waterhouse as a sort of final salute to his aunt. By the time he arrived it was dark. The house had been cleaned, but still had a damp smell. It felt cold and lonely. He walked up to the Agricultural, forgetting they didn't serve food and then had a second pint of beer in the Fox and Hounds to wash down a plate of soggy steak pie and chips. Returning to the Waterhouse, he noticed an envelope had been pushed under the door. The message read: *Meet me tomorrow morning at six at the barn in Lovers' Walk.* It was signed *Jenny.*

Lovers' Walk was a small valley on the other side of the village which was reached by a footpath that ran the three miles from Freasby to Heby. It was formed by three brooks, which comprised the source of the River Cater, coming together at the head of the valley. It was of interest to local historians because it was bounded on one side by a low hill and on the other by the earthworks of a Norman castle which had protected the nearby twelfth-century Freasby Abbey. The stream had been diverted by the fort to make a small moat before disappearing underground. It emerged a few hundred yards further down the valley before running into a large medieval fish pond close to the abbey. At some distance from the road, it was rarely frequented. The banks of the valley were quite overgrown with hawthorn scrub and a mixture of mature oak and ash which hung over the vale, casting a dappled shade on the grass. Redstarts were a summer visitor. Running east to west, it offered the most beautiful sunsets and sunrises. It had a magical quality, and had been a popular trysting place for courting couples. At the eastern end was a dilapidated, three-sided stone shelter with a slate roof, which was used to store fodder and as protection for the sheep against the winter wind.

As Joe walked into the valley he was struck by the beautiful morning sky. The rich russet of the sun's rays cast a golden shadow over the scattered banks of high cloud, creating a new world in the heavens. Taking a deep breath of the fresh, crisp air and listening to the glorious chorus of blackbirds, finches and tits, he realised that spring was now in full cry while he had been mouldering in London. As he sat in the shelter and watched the brook chattering on its way to the distant sea. he felt the sense of alienation that had been with him for the last fortnight lift from his mind and depart in the breeze.

'You look thoughtful.'

He turned and saw Jenny, dressed in her riding outfit, leading her horse towards the shelter. She tied it up against a post set in the wall and took off her hat, giving her head a shake to loosen her hair. She smiled.

'You came then,' she said.

'Didn't you expect me to?'

'I wasn't very friendly at our last meeting.'

Joe shrugged.

'You remember this place?' she asked, sitting down on a bale of straw.

'How could I forget? What did happen anyway? Why did I ruin your life?'

'Oh, I didn't mean it. I had just had a row with David, my husband, and I took out my feelings on you.'

She got up and went over to him stroking his face with her whip.

'You know I did love you. I think eleven-year-olds can fall in love, don't you? That time when… you know, when we played doctors and nurses, only you didn't pass your exams, what I didn't know was that Billy, my brother, was watching us. Peeping through that hole in the wall. See, it's still there. He told my dad, which was bad enough because he beat me to a pulp, but Billy also told everyone at school which made my life hell. Everybody thought you were stuck-up so they teased me about that and they also called me all sorts of names. It was so bad Dad had to move me to another school. I was miserable. Then when you abandoned me I thought my life might as well come to an end. I even tried to kill myself once, and all the sympathy I got was another beating from Dad. Then I tried to run away and he beat me for that, sadistic bastard. I hated him. I was so glad when he drank himself to death. So in a way, you did ruin my life, although it was Dad really, I suppose.' She smiled at him. 'A typical story of country folk.'

'I'm sorry,' he said lamely.

'Oh it's all in the past now. But that's not why I asked you to come either. You're being ripped off over this sale.'

'Why?' It seems a good price to me. Louise, my girlfriend, doesn't normally get these things wrong.'

'Carter can get planning permission for the twelve-acre field next to village. He'll knock the Waterhouse down and build a little village. It's worth a fortune.'

'How do you know?'

'His builder told me.'

'Why?'

'Pillow talk,'

'Oh,' Joe replied with a smile.

'It hasn't worked out between David and me,' he drinks and then he hits me, just like Dad did, so I have affairs.'

'Why tell me?' Joe asked curiously. 'You would stand to gain in time, wouldn't you?'

'For one thing, I've decided to leave David and move to Leicester. I did some secretarial training a few years ago and it's about time I earned myself a living, but mainly I'm telling you as a favour to your friend Walter. He and his wife have always been very kind to me. Haven't judged me like most people in this god-awful village. And now I must go and get the children ready for school. Be good, and if you do sell make sure you get a decent price. I'd hate to see Fred make a killing. Oh, and talking of killing, you might ask him how the tree came down that caused the Waterhouse to flood.' With a farewell kiss on his cheek, she mounted her horse and trotted away.

26

By the time Joe arrived at the solicitor's Carter and Louise were both waiting. Mrs Morgan smiled at him.

'Good morning Mr Landseer. This shouldn't take a moment. These are the papers you need to sign, one set to complete the transfer of the property under the terms of the will, and then the exchange of contracts.'

Joe took the papers and shuffled through them.

'Mrs Morgan, I wonder if I could have a word with Mr Carter and Louise in private?'

'I do have another appointment at 11.30,' Mrs Morgan said as she showed her clients into an anteroom.

'This property is worth a great deal more than eight hundred thousand pounds, isn't it Mr Carter?' Joe said as the door closed behind them.

'How do you mean?'

'Twelve acres. Quarter-acres plots. Let's say forty houses at two to four hundred thousand each. Fifty percent profit; I would say you should clear six million on this deal.' Joe stared at Carter. who returned his look with a stony gaze.

'Joe, what are you talking about?' Louise asked.

'He can get planning permission. He's going to build Cartersville right in the middle of the Waterhouse. All that stuff about keeping the property as it is and respecting my aunt's wishes, that was all crap, wasn't it?'

'How did you find out?'

'It doesn't matter. It's true, isn't it?'

'I may be able to get planning permission, that's true, but I can't be certain. I'm taking a risk. That place isn't worth half what I am offering you in the state it's in, especially after the flood.'

'And whose fault was that, I wonder?'

'What do you mean by that?'

'I've heard that tree didn't come down of its own accord, which makes me wonder who was most likely to profit by making the Waterhouse uninhabitable.'

'That is a very serious accusation young man.'

'And one that's not far from the mark, I would guess,' Joe replied, feeling suddenly very angry at the thought that this man in all likelihood nearly killed him.

They stared at each other for a moment before Carter averted his gaze.

'Anyway, I've decided not to sell,' Joe continued.

'What?!' Carter and Louise said together.

Joe shuffled awkwardly. 'The deal was that you would look after the place. Keep it as it was.'

'Don't be so naive,' Louise said crossly. 'That's romantic nonsense and you know it.'

'Now let's all calm down a bit,' Carter said, becoming businesslike. 'I'll tell you what. You're quite right, I do hope to get planning permission. So here is what I'll do. You agree to sell me the house and land. If I get to build the houses we'll form a partnership; – you, me and the builder – and share the profits equally. If I can't get permission, I'll still buy the property for eight hundred. It could make you a rich man. I can't say fairer than that.'

'Joe, that's brilliant,' Louise said enthusiastically.

'I'll get Morgan to draw up a memorandum of understanding; that should cover it until we can get the paperwork fixed properly.'

'I'm still not selling,' Joe said defiantly.

'I think Joe and I need to have a word together,' Louise said to Carter ushering him out of the room. 'Ask the solicitor to write that memorandum.'

'What do you mean, you're not selling?' she said, turning on Joe. 'Are you mad? We'd be rich.'

'It doesn't seem right. The man is a crook. Practically a murderer. If I don't sell, I could still develop the land in the future and keep all the profits to myself.'

'You're upset about falling in the river.'

'Well so would you be if you saw your life flashing before you like I did. Besides, I like it here. I like the country and I owe it to my aunt. She kept that place for me. I should respect that.'

'God Joe, you make me so cross sometimes.' Louise said, her face becoming red with anger. 'Who knows what will happen to planning laws in the future, and what about me? If you think I'm going to shut myself up in this hell hole you've got another think coming, and there is no way I'm commuting to Leicester at weekends until you get over this stupid, premature, mid-life crisis of yours. I tell you Joe, she continued, having worked herself up into a pitch of fury, 'it's either me or the Waterhouse. Either you sign that letter or that's the last you'll see of me.' With which ultimatum, she stormed out of the room.

Joe heard her clattering down the stairs and slam the street door. He looked out of the window and watched her walk down the street. Then he turned and went back into the office, his mind made up.

An hour later, Joe was sitting in the kitchen of the Waterhouse when Louise's car skidded to halt outside. He opened the door and Louise stormed in.

'Sign this bloody memorandum or I'm out of here for good,' she said furiously, flourishing a piece of paper.

'Don't be so melodramatic Louise. I'm not going to sign it. Not until I've had some more time to think about it. I don't know why you're being like this. Apart from Carter trying to rip me off, he almost got me killed.'

'Killed?!' she said scornfully. 'Now who is being melodramatic? God, you make me sick sometimes with your hypochondria and your phobia of water. If I know anything, you were probably as much at risk of drowning as if you had stepped in a puddle.'

Joe turned red with anger and slammed his fist down on the kitchen table. Unfortunately anger was an emotion that embarrassed him. This inhibited the downswing of his arm, so that instead of the intended deafening crash he produced a timorous knock.

'Well I'm really quaking at my knees after that demonstration,' Louise said sarcastically. 'You know, that's the trouble with you Joe. Inhibited. Can't let yourself go. Somebody floods your house, and instead of acting like a man, punching him on the nose and then buying him a drink, you go all high and mighty about it. Well, I'm fed up with you. Jamie thought you were stand-offish and he was right. You're like a melting icicle. Stiff, cold and dripping.' Louise smirked at her metaphor. 'You go and get the sack and it's as if the world has come to an end. Get some backbone, can't you?'

She sat down in a chair by the stove. 'Look,' she continued in a softer tone, 'I hate getting cross. We always seem to be rowing these days. Let's not fight over this. All you need to do is sign the paper and then we can go back to London and forget the Waterhouse ever existed.'

'I'm not signing and that's that. In fact, I'm not coming back to London either,' Joe said firmly. 'I think it will do us good to have some time apart. You're right, I haven't been much fun recently. Perhaps if we see less of each other for a while we'll enjoy each other's company more. As for that wanker Jamie, it's a compliment to be insulted by him.'

'It's that girl isn't it?' Louise said, standing up and coming over to face him, 'If you betray me for that slut I'll kill you.' To emphasise this point she grasped a large, serrated bread knife that was on the kitchen table.

Joe, moved a few steps sideways to interpose a chair between them. 'What girl?' Joe said defensively.

'Don't act all innocent with me. The one Felicity caught you fooling about with. I might have known. You want her to get the money, not me. Well, I'm not standing for it. I tell you Joe Landseer, I'll screw you for every penny if you try and do me out of this money. By God, I will. Jamie said you would try and keep it all to yourself.'

'Don't talk crap,' Joe said, getting heated in his turn. 'I don't give a damn about the money, and what's all this "Jamie this" and "Jamie that"? I don't know why you're listening to a guy who can't keep his todger in his trousers for longer than it takes to say, "Clap Clinic"'.

'At least it's all in one piece.'

Joe, sensitive about his circumcised status, pursed his lips.

'I'm sorry,' Louise said, realising she had gone too far, 'that was below the belt.' She then spoiled her contrition by letting out a suppressed giggle at the involuntary pun.

'How do you know anyway?' Joe asked, the implications of her insult sinking in.

Louise blushed. 'Somebody said,' she stammered.

'Somebody?! Who?' he asked coming up close to her. 'You've slept with him, haven't you? That night when I was in hospital. 'You bastard. There I was, dying for all you cared, and you were humping that cut-price Lothario. Come on, admit it.'

'Well, what if I did? It was your fault anyway,' she said

defiantly. 'I was lonely, you being up here. And I was jealous of that woman.' Whereupon, she started to cry.

Joe felt no sympathy, only dejection that their relationship had come to such a sordid end. 'That is just so much bullshit, Louise,' he said in a measured tone, gently prising the knife away from her grasp. 'There is no other woman and you know it. Save your tears. It's all over. We've been drifting apart for months. You like London and sewage rats like Jamie Levitt and I don't. Simple as that.'

'Fuck you, Joe Landseer,' she said, stalking out.

27

Three weeks later, on the first Saturday in May, the Freasby Spring Fair was held on the village green to celebrate May Day. The fete had taken place for as long as anyone could remember. There were records in the County Office in Leicester suggesting it had first been held to commemorate the coronation of Charles II, the parliamentarians having frowned on this sort of thing. However, an amateur local historian had found reference to the fair in the fifteenth-century diary of one of the abbots from Freasby Abbey. He even claimed to have found evidence of a horse fair in Freasby getting in the way of some witch-burning in Felton during the reign of Stephen and Matilda. Suffice to say the Spring Fair had been going on for a long time.

As befitted it's ancestry, it was grander than most of the May Day village fetes and possessed a degree of local fame, not to say notoriety, which attracted crowds from Felton and Leicester. There was a maypole dance which was led by the Spring Queen. Traditionally she was chosen from amongst the teenage virgins of the village although it had been necessary to relax this rule somewhat in recent years. There was a troop of morris dancers, whose membership largely consisted of local young farmers. Their performance, which was seldom foot-perfect at the best of times, had a tendency, as a result of refreshments taken at frequent intervals from the Agricultural Inn, to become increasingly erratic as the afternoon wore on. The disorganisation in their choreography invariably attracted the attention of certain members of the audience from the rougher areas of Felton who themselves had enjoyed the inn's hospitality. Instead of greeting the morris dancers' performance with the gentle applause, appropriate to such an occasion, questions were raised regarding the sexual orientation of the young farmers. This not infrequently led to both parties ending up in the village pond. Indeed once, there had been a near riot, to the extent that the event had been brought to the attention of the Chief Constable. This had resulted in the farmers being banished from membership of the Morris-Dancing Society of England, a humiliation which did not appear to greatly cramp their style. There were also the usual entertainment's such as throwing the welly, a coconut shy, a fortune teller, a sheepdog trial and a tug-of-war competition between teams from Freasby and the surrounding villages. Various stalls ringed the green, including a plant stall, several selling home-made jams and pastries, a guess-the-weight-of-the-cake competition, and the organisational hub of a treasure trail.

However, the centre piece of the Freasby Spring Fair was the competition for the heaviest pig, and it was here that Joe found Walter, at midday, dressed in his Sunday best, waiting anxiously for the event to start. The rules were simple. All entrants needed to have been born and raised within a three-mile radius of the village green. The winner, good treatment and grooming being taken for granted, was the pig that weighed in the heaviest. There were five pigs entered. To the layperson they all looked vast, but an expert eye could have seen immediately that the outcome of the competition was between Harry and Donald, the pig owned by Carter. Carter was leaning against the pens chatting to Walter, but walked off when Joe appeared. Joe had been press-ganged into making up the numbers of the Morris Dancers and Walter gave him a curious look as he walked up in his costume of a green shirt and leggings complete with hat and bells.

'Don't say a word,' Joe warned taking his hat off. 'Are you going to win?'

'He would have walked it 'cept for that soaking he got,' Walter said, with unusual animation. 'Put him off his food for two days, that did. Now it'll be touch-and-go.'

'You always say that Walter,' Stan, who was standing nearby, chipped in. 'Hasn't stopped you winning for four out of the last five years.'

'That as maybe,' Walter said gravely. 'We shall see soon enough anyhow. 'By the way lad,' he continued turning to Joe. 'I think I've got some good news for you.' And he handed Joe a piece of paper.

It was a copy of a letter from DeLuca to the university, setting out the terms of his endowment of a chair. There was a paragraph stipulating that Alice must be employed as a research assistant.

'Walter, this is brilliant. How did you get this? Does she know?'

'Doubt it. Only posted yesterday. Now hold your peace. They are about to start.'

With four pigs weighed in, Donald was in the lead at twenty-six stone, three pounds and two ounces. There was a gasp and a ripple of applause as the weight was announced. Then Harry waddled onto the weighing machine. Walter gripped the sides of the pen tightly. The old-fashioned scales swung round. Twenty-six stone, twenty-seven stone, finally settling just above twenty-six stone. Walter and Joe strained their eyes. There was a tense hush. Twenty-six stone, three pounds and one ounce. Harry shifted his weight and the pointer moved two and fro for a few seconds before settling again. Twenty-six stone, three pounds and three ounces the judge announced quickly. I name Harry Chevanage-Bramley the winner. A cheer went up and much shaking of hands and backslapping ensued with Walter wearing a grin as broad as his back. He was handed an envelope containing the two-hundred-and-fifty-pound cash prize, and Harry was led away.

'Where are they taking Harry?' Joe asked Walter.

'He's going to the butcher's at Tigby. Get him ready for the feast tonight.'

'What?!' Joe asked in alarm. 'He's going to be killed?'

'That's the tradition,' Walter replied. Winning pig provides the meat for the roast. It's grand. The pig on a spit, country music, lots of dancing. You'll see.'

'But you can't do it Walter,' Joe pleaded, 'not to Harry. He saved my life. Look, I'll buy him back. Let Carter's pig get eaten.'

'Sorry lad. That's the tradition. You'll get used to our country ways soon enough.'

No I damn well won't, Joe thought, beginning to regret his move to the country, although in truth he had enjoyed himself these last few weeks – getting the animals back, starting to do up the house, planting some potatoes while spring came into full sway. He felt lonely though. He couldn't stop thinking of Alice. He had tried to contact her, but he had realised how little he knew about her. He had managed to find her university email address but had received only out-of-office notifications in response to his messages. He didn't have her postal address and he had managed to lose her phone number. Finally he had written her a letter via the university, but hadn't received a reply. He kicked a can of Coke disconsolately and decided to go home.

At the edge of the green he felt a tug on his arm. He turned round to see Jenny smiling at him.

'Very smart, I must say,' she said sardonically, admiring his outfit.

'I thought you'd given up on the country?'

'I promised to take the children to the fair. You look fed up.'

'It's Harry. I can't believe they are going to eat him.'

'Oh that. Follow me.'

She led him to the entrance of a lane at the back of the Agricultural. At the other end of the lane he saw Walter handing over some money to the butcher who had taken Harry away. Walter then led Harry up the road towards the village.

'It's part of the tradition,' Jenny explained. 'We all pretend that the winner is eaten, but the owner usually buys back the champion pig and the butcher substitutes it for another one. The champion duly comes back next year under another name. Harry has won it for the last three years now. He was called Humphrey last year. Mind you, I think he'll be hard put to it with Fred's pig next year. I don't seem to have cheered you up much,' she continued with a concerned look. 'If you are still cross about me exposing you to the elements the other week I would be happy to make things up to you,' she continued with a suggestive look.

'Another time perhaps,' Joe said politely.

'Give me a call. See you around.'

Joe watched her walk back to the fair. Then, turning towards the churchyard, he ambled along the footpath back towards the Waterhouse. It was early afternoon. The sky was cloudless and it was warm enough for Joe to feel hot in his morris-man uniform. The hay meadow was a profusion of flowers. The buttercups cast a yellow sheen over the field, contrasting with the sprinkled pink patches of lady's smock which danced sinuously in the breeze. The tiny white flowers of the mouse-ear, encouraged to peep out from their tightly clasped leaves by the spring sun, spread around his feet, largely hidden by the multitude of grasses, now starting to flourish as the days lengthened. Joe bent down and picked a couple of blades of grass, holding them to his nose to smell the freshness of the season. He looked towards the house and admired the willows that surrounded the Waterhouse, which were now in full leaf, hiding the buildings from view. Only the oaks and ashes were yet to show their summer coats, and they stood out as if dead, their bare branches contrasting sharply with the rich greenery of the hedges at their feet. From the top branch of an ash, a blackbird sang it's sibilant call before swooping down towards one of the barns.

Joe felt his spirits lift. He basked in the glory of spring reflected in the warming rays of the afternoon sun and sensed a profound conviction that this was where he belonged. He would find happiness here amongst the chorus of birds, the verdant pastures bordered with hawthorn, and the changing seasons rich with varied charms. It was his home, and he was content. Or almost content, for his thoughts of Alice gnawed at his sense of well-being. He had to find her.

28

When Joe got back from the fair he checked his mailbox and carried his newspaper and a couple of circulars into the kitchen. As he put the pile onto the table, he noticed a post-card, showing a picture of a Devon village, that had got caught between the pages of the newspaper. He picked it up and turned it over. *Getting married Saturday 3.00pm. London Road Registry Office. Come and wish me luck?* It was signed, *All my love, Alice.*

Joe sat down heavily. That was today. He loooked at his watch. Five to two. She would be out of reach in an hour. Despair entered his heart, leaving him cold and exhausted. It was only now that he realised how much he had been hoping that he and Alice would get together. He had never felt like this about Louise. This was different. He looked again at the postcard. How could she do this? She didn't love Andrew, she loved him, he was sure of it. He read the message again and again. *All my love*, he thought. *That's it.* The postcard was telling him to rescue her. If only she knew about the job. He must get to her before she was married. It was thirteen miles to Leicester. He would take the Land Rover.

He dashed out of the kitchen, running to the garage. Then he remembered the Land Rover was being serviced. He tried not to panic. *Think clearly. There must be a way.* Who had a car? Jenny, but she might have gone. He could go up to the village and spend half an hour looking for her and be no better off. He could hitch-hike. Too uncertain. He could run. Thirteen miles in one hour. Not very likely. He looked around wildly, hoping for inspiration, and there, peeking out of the corner of his eye, was a flash of red. It was the work of a moment to unhook the trailer and then he was off, full throttle, Leicester bound, sitting astride his aged, but trusty Massey Ferguson 135.

Top speed was twenty miles an hour. Joe calculated that as long as he could find the registry office and there weren't any major traffic jams he could make it. A tractor on the road was commonplace in the country and even dressed as a morris dancer Joe barely warranted a glance as he chugged through the streets of the commuter villages of Fileby and Thressington. It was only when he reached the outskirts of Leicester and travelled up the Felton road that he started receiving some very curious glances from the largely Asian population that lived in the area. However, Joe was oblivious to his appearance, his concentration focused on gaining every possible advantage in his desire to reach the London Road. Weaving his tractor in and out of the traffic he used his lack of concern about inflicting damage to ruthless advantage, mercilessly cutting up cars at roundabouts and traffic lights, giving full vent to his horn in response to the angry gestures of their drivers.

He knew that London Road was a main artery that ran past the railway station south out of Leicester although he had no idea of the whereabouts of the registry office. As he waited for the traffic lights outside the station to turn, he looked at his watch. Ten to three. The lights turned yellow and he blared his horn to encourage the car in front, a blue Vauxhall, to get going. Then in frustration, when it didn't move despite the lights turning green, he let out the clutch and gave the car a nudge with the front loader. This was a mistake. Instead of driving off, two men in suits got out and started to walk towards him. Joe looked behind, but he was trapped by another car. While Alice was getting married, he was going to be a victim of road rage. He looked down at the man on his right and found himself staring at a police badge.

'Good afternoon, sir. Inspector Harkins. Do you have a licence for this vehicle?'

'Officer. I'm terribly sorry. I didn't mean to hit your bumper. My foot slipped on the clutch.'

'Quite, sir. Now, if you don't mind just stepping down so we can ask you a few questions.'

'But you don't understand. I have to get to a wedding. My wedding. London Road Registry Office. My fiancée and I are morris dancers. That's why I'm dressed like this. It's at three o'clock. My car broke down and I had to borrow this tractor. You've got to help me.'

The policeman, a thin-faced man in his forties, smiled.

'We've got a right joker here,' he said to his partner. 'Sounds like he's already been dipping into the bubbly, doesn't it? Now sir, if you don't mind, I've got this little bag I would like you to breathe into and we haven't got all day.'

When the police had finally decided that Joe was sober and legally allowed to drive around the streets of Leicester in a tractor they let him go. It was five o'clock and he left in a state of utter dejection. The registry office was closed and deserted. The drive home was about the most miserable hour of Joe's life. He was crushed. His one chance of love had disappeared while he kicked his heels in a police station.

He parked the tractor in the drive and, with barely a nod to Trigger who gave him a welcoming neigh, he went into the kitchen. The house, which still bore the scars of the flood and carried the odour of damp and mould, was far from welcoming. He slumped down in an armchair and started to feel sorry for himself. For the first time he wondered whether he had done the right thing in not selling to Carter. Hercule came and rubbed himself against his leg. Joe picked him up and putting him on his knee, tickled him behind the ears.

'Well old chap, what are we going to do now?' he asked rhetorically.

In reply, Hercule settled himself down for a snooze. Joe thought this was not such a bad idea and closed his eyes, feeling worn out.

He came out of his doze to the sensation of being kissed. This was a rather enjoyable reverie he thought, keeping his eyes closed to better enjoy the sensation, pouting his lips to invite another caress. To his delight, another kiss came, this time a more complete sensation. *That felt real*, he thought and opened his eyes. Alice smiled down at him.

'I am assuming this is a most wonderful dream,' he said, pulling her into an embrace which displaced a rather irritated Hercule. They kissed again, with unbounded joy.

'After I sent the postcard to you I realised I couldn't go through with it. It would never have worked out. I came up to Leicester to tell Andrew and got both your letter and the one from DeLuca this morning. I've been plucking up the courage to come over ever since. Isn't it wonderful? Why did he change his mind do you think?

'No idea. Walter is the man to ask. It seems there is a lot more to Mr Bramley than being a champion pig breeder.'

'I guess so,' Alice agreed. 'I can't believe you're going to be a farmer.'

'Can't believe in the "You'll be completely useless" sense, or in the "You must be mad" sort of way?'

'Can't believe meaning I have complete confidence you will turn the Waterhouse into a wildlife paradise.'

'I'll need lots of help of course. Paradises don't come easy.'

'You means squires need their peasants,' Alice said with a smile.

'As long as they are careful where they put their forks,' Joe responded with a grin. 'Of course, what squires really need is someone to keep them warm at night.'

'I think that could be arranged.'

'Actually, I'm feeling a bit on the chilly side right now.'

'We can't have that,' Alice said suggestively, running her hand through Joe's hair.

'Alice?' Joe said, after another lingering kiss.

'Mm?' she said dreamily.

'I think I love you.'

'Joe?' she replied, kissing him gently on the tip of his nose.

'Mm?'

'I think I love you too.'